Whist... I'll Come

"She's really happy," said Sally. "She's really grateful to us for taking her."

Mum glanced back at her in the driving mirror.

"I dread to think what your dad's going to say."

"He can't say anything," said Sally. "He told us ... we could have a dozen if we wanted. Anyway –" she placed an arm protectively over Beth's shoulders – "We're not giving her back, whatever he says. She's our dog, now!"

Whistle and I'll Come

Jean Ure

Scholastic Children's Books,
Commonwealth House, 1–19 New Oxford Street,
London WC1A 1NU, UK
a division of Scholastic Ltd
London ~ New York ~ Toronto ~ Sydney ~ Auckland

First published by Scholastic Ltd, 1997
This edition first published by Scholastic Ltd, 1998

Text copyright © Jean Ure, 1997

ISBN 0 590 11255 4

Typeset by DP Photosetting, Aylesbury, Bucks
Printed by Cox & Wyman Ltd, Reading, Berks

10 9 8 7 6 5 4 3 2 1

The right of Jean Ure to be identified as the author of this work has
been asserted by her in accordance with the Copyright, Designs and
Patents Act, 1988.

This book is for Last Chance Rescue Centre, Edenbridge, Kent. It is also dedicated to the memory of William, "the best of dogs".

Chapter One

Sally's mum had always said, "As soon as we have a proper garden, we can go out and get ourselves a dog."

Well, they had a proper garden now, and it was a big one, too. Not much in the way of flower beds but lots of trees and grass and wild bushes, which was how Mum liked it. Trees and bushes were good for the birds, Mum said; and all the tangled undergrowth would provide shelter for small animals such as mice and hedgehogs.

"We might even get foxes, if we're lucky."

"Wouldn't foxes hurt the dog?" said Sally.

"No! Foxes are quiet, shy creatures. They don't want any trouble."

"What about Oscar?" said Susan.

Susan was Sally's sister. She was fourteen and thought herself practically grown up. Oscar was the cat. He was almost twelve, which was a year older than Sally.

"Oscar can look after himself," said Mum. "Look at the size of him! Great lumping creature. He'd see a fox off in no time."

It was true that Oscar was no ordinary cat. He was a stripy ginger tom with a head like a big furry football and a tail that could puff itself out like a lavatory brush.

"I pity any fox that tangled with him!" said Mum. "Now, let's decide what sort of dog we want."

It was Mum and Sally who were the dog people. Mum had had dogs (and cats, and rabbits, and hamsters and guinea pigs) when she was a girl. Dad had always lived in a flat, in the middle of town, and hadn't had any animals at all. He said that if Mum wanted a dog, "Then I suppose you'll have to have one."

All Mum's married life she had wanted a dog, but they had never had a garden before;

just a scrubby bit of back yard without any grass. Now they had so much garden they could almost have kept a horse – but Dad drew the line at horses.

"I don't know why you can't stick to guinea pigs," he said.

"Dad!" cried Sally. "You promised! We don't want guinea pigs, we want a dog. Don't we, Mum?"

"I'm afraid we do," said Mum.

"What about Susan? What does she have to say?"

"Don't ask me," said Susan.

Susan, just at the moment, couldn't have cared less. She was more interested in her boyfriend, a spotty youth called Justin, who had thin gangly arms that hung down to his knees (which were knobbly). Sally couldn't think what her sister saw in him, but Mum wouldn't let her tease. She said, "You'll be just the same when you're Sue's age." Sally bet she wouldn't! She'd sooner have a dog than a spotty boyfriend any day of the week.

She and Mum borrowed a dog book from the library and pored over it together.

"When I was young," said Mum, "we used to have a Beardie."

"What's a Beardie?" said Sally.

"A bearded collie . . . he was called Walter. He was a real character. Into everything! We used to knock around together all the time, me and Walter. He was my playmate."

"So shall we have one of those, then?"

Mum shook her head, regretfully.

"I promised your dad something small. See if we can find something small!"

They found Yorkies and Westies and sausage dogs and Scotties. They found Sealyhams and Pekes and tiny toy terriers.

"I wish we could have a St Bernard," said Sally.

"No way!" Mum laughed. "Your dad would have a fit. How about one of these little chaps?" Mum pointed to a picture of a small cheeky dog with sticky-up ears. "A chihuahua."

"Chee-wa-wa." Sally repeated it, thoughtfully. "Mmm . . . I s'pose."

"You can't get much smaller than a chihuahua."

"I'd rather have a Great Dane."

"Yes, well, I'd rather have a German Shepherd, but Dad's nervous enough about the idea of a dog as it is."

"Is he frightened?" said Sally.

"No, he's not frightened. It just worries him because he's never had one before."

"Nor have I," said Sally, "but I'm not worried."

"That's because you're a real dog lover. You've caught it from me. You probably wouldn't turn a hair if we brought a Rottweiler into the house. But your dad needs something small and gentle ... just to start him off with. Once he's got used to the idea —"

"What?" said Sally.

A little smile played on Mum's lips. "We shall see! Go on looking at the dog book."

"What about a Labrador?" said Sally. "They're nice."

"They are, they're gorgeous. But too big! Far too big! What about a Cairn terrier? They're game little dogs."

"What about a Huskie?"

"Not suitable. What about a Norfolk?"

"Oh, Mum! What about a Chow?"

"Chows aren't as cuddly as they look. They're not an easy dog. And anyway –"

"*Too big.*"

"Much too big."

"So what about a –"

"What about this, what about that … you know what I think?" Mum closed the book with a sudden snap. "I think we oughtn't to be buying a pedigree dog at all. I think we ought to be going to a rescue centre. All those poor animals that have been thrown out or ill-treated … just waiting for someone to come along and love them and give them a good home. I think that's what we ought to be doing."

"Yes," said Sally. "*I* think that's what we ought to be doing, too."

"First thing tomorrow," said Mum, "I shall start ringing round the rescue centres."

Next day, when Mum dropped her off at school, Sally whispered, "Don't forget about the rescue centres!"

"I won't," said Mum. "I promise."

Sally spent all day in school dreaming about the dog that she and Mum were going to rescue. It had to be something small, because of Dad being nervous. And it had to be something young, because of not being too set in its ways. And it had to be a bitch, because of bitches being easier to control, or at least that was what Mum said. Which was probably true, thought Sally. All the really *worst* behaved people in her class were boys, especially one called Bernard Roberts. Bernard Roberts was the naughtiest boy in the whole school.

At breaktime she told her best friend Gemma about her and Mum getting a dog. Gemma wailed, "Oh, you are so lucky!"

Gemma's mum wouldn't let her have a dog; she said there wasn't anyone at home all day to look after it. And she wouldn't let her have a cat because of living on the main road. Poor old Gemma had to make do with gerbils.

"What sort of dog are you going to get? A *big* dog?"

"Small dog. We're going to rescue one.

We're going to a rescue centre."

"I couldn't bear to go to a rescue centre," said Gemma. "Imagine all those poor dogs you'll have to leave behind ... all sitting in their cages, watching you."

"I know," said Sally. Mum had already warned her that it wouldn't be easy. "But if everyone felt like that, then none of them would ever get rescued."

It was Dad who came to pick Sally up from school that afternoon. Sometimes he did that when he stopped work early.

"I thought we'd drive home the long way and pop in to the DIY," said Dad. "That OK?"

Normally, Sally would have been only too happy to drive home the long way and pop in to the DIY. She liked doing things with her dad. Today she just wanted to get home and find out if Mum had kept her promise.

"That all right?" said Dad.

"Yes," said Sally.

"You quite sure?" said Dad.

"Mm!" Sally did her best to sound enthusiastic. Dad would be hurt if he thought she didn't want to go with him.

"It'll only take five minutes. I just want to pick up a few tools."

Of course it didn't take five minutes because Dad in a DIY shop was as bad as Susan in a clothes shop. (Or Mum and Sally at a rescue centre?) By the time they arrived home, Mum was in a flap and wondering where they'd got to.

"It was Dad," said Sally. "We went to the DIY."

"Oh." Mum nodded. "I see."

"He only went in for a few tools."

"And came out with half the shop. *I* know!"

Dad grinned. He looked like a naughty schoolboy. A bit like Bernard Roberts.

Dad went off to put his new tools in the tool shed while Mum took the plates out of the oven and yelled upstairs to Susan that tea was ready.

"Mum!" Sally dabbled her hands under the tap and smeared them down the roller towel. Washing hands was such a bore. "Mum, did you do it? Did you r—?"

"Sh!" Mum placed a finger to her lips. "I'll tell you after tea. I want your dad to be in a good mood!"

Mum's eyes were sparkling with excitement. She also looked a bit like Bernard Roberts. What had she been up to? Maybe she had found a Great Dane...

Tea was Dad's absolute all-time favourite: egg and chips. That was suspicious in itself. Dad was only ever allowed to eat egg and chips on special occasions because of something called cholesterol.

"Why have we got this?" said Susan. "I thought you said chips were bad for you. I thought you s—"

"Never mind what I said," said Mum. "You get it down you. A plate of chips never hurt anyone just once in a while."

"I don't want to get spots!" whined Susan. She didn't mind Justin getting spots: great big yellow-headed things that always looked on the point of bursting. Ugh! Sally shuddered. Imagine being kissed by that. Dogs were far nicer. She wouldn't have the least objection to being kissed by a dog.

When they had finished eating their egg and chips, and Oscar was crouched in secretive fashion on the draining board, cleaning the plates, Mum, very carelessly, said: "I rang a rescue centre today. End of the Road, near Edenbridge."

There was a silence. Then Dad, who was reading one of the manuals which had come with his new tools, said "Mm?" just to show that he was paying attention (though he wasn't really, Sally could tell). Susan was examining herself in the mirror for spots. She didn't even bother to say "Mm." Only Sally leaned forward, bright-eyed and eager.

"I told them we were looking for a dog. A small dog. Preferably a bitch. Not too old. They said they had a couple," said Mum. "Two little girls, about eighteen months."

Sally waited, breathlessly.

"The only thing is," said Mum, "they want to re-home them as a pair. They've been brought up together and they don't want to separate them. So I was thinking," said Mum, "that really and truly two dogs wouldn't be any more trouble than one. In fact they'd probably be less. They could amuse each other and keep each other company when we went out. We wouldn't have to worry about leaving one on its own.

"Not only that," said Mum, "but when you think about it, a dog is a pack animal. It needs others of its own kind. It's not really fair just having one. Especially not when it's been brought up with another. I mean, those two little girls..."

There was a pause. Mum giggled, nervously.

"It would be positively cruel to part them. And they wouldn't let us, anyway. Whoever takes one, has to take the other."

"You mean we're going to have *two*?" squeaked Sally.

"What?" Dad slowly lowered his manual. "What did you say?"

"We're going to have two!" cried Sally.

"Now, look here—" began Dad.

"They're only small!" Mum said it pleadingly. "Just two very tiny little dogs."

"Not like Great Danes," said Sally, trying to be helpful.

"We weren't going to have a Great Dane! We were going to have *one* small one."

"Oh, Alistair!" said Mum.

Mum's bottom lip quivered. Dad made a noise that sounded like "Hrrmph!" and turned away. There was a pause.

"Dad bought *oodles* of tools today," said Sally. "Oodles and *oodles*."

"Tools are useful," said Susan. She often sided with Dad rather than with Mum and Sally.

"So are dogs useful!" retorted Sally.

"No, they're not. Not ordinary pet ones."

"Yes, they are! They keep you fit and healthy. I read it somewhere."

"They'll pee on the lawn," said Susan.

"We haven't got a lawn!" You couldn't call a tangle of grass and weeds and wild flowers a *lawn*.

"We could have one," said Susan.

"Well, we don't have one! We'd rather have dogs."

"That's typical of you," said Susan. "*Selfish*. What about Dad and me? I suppose it doesn't matter what we want?"

"When did you ever want a lawn? When did—"

"Girls! Please," begged Mum. "Don't make it worse. It's my fault. I shouldn't have said we'd have them without consulting your father. I'll ring up first thing tomorrow and tell them."

"Tell them what?" Sally's voice quavered.

"Tell them we can't," said Mum.

"Oh, Mum!" begged Sally.

"Hush!" said Mum. "Be fair. It's extremely good of Dad to say we can even have one. Don't start making a fuss or he'll change his mind and won't let us have any."

"Oh, now, come on! For goodness' sake!" Dad's face broke into a reluctant grin. "Don't make me out to be some kind of ogre. When have I ever said no to anything you really seriously wanted? I don't care how many dogs you have! Have half a dozen if it's going to make you happy. You've waited long enough."

"Ali!" Mum flew at him. "You're an angel!"

"No, I'm not," said Dad. "I'm just a poor weak fool whose life is ruled by domineering women. When are you planning to get these dogs, anyway?"

"I said we'd go down on Saturday."

Dad looked alarmed. "All of us?"

"Just me and Sally. Unless, of course, you'd like to come too?"

"Not me," said Dad. "I'm going to be playing with my new tools."

"And I'm going into town," said Susan.

Sally didn't know why she'd bothered telling them that. No one had asked her to come.

"I suppose I'll be expected to go round the garden," grumbled Dad, "and make sure the fence is secure."

"No, no! You don't have to do a thing. I'll see to the fence," said Mum.

"You?" Dad reached out for his glass of water. "I wouldn't trust you an inch when it comes to anything practical. I shall see to it."

Mum winked at Sally across the table. Sally giggled. At that moment, Oscar nosed a plate off the draining board and sat complacently watching as it smashed to pieces on the floor.

"That cat!" screamed Mum.

Susan raced across the kitchen and scooped him up.

"Poor Oscar! He doesn't know his home is going to be invaded by nasty horrid canines."

"Don't you worry about Oscar," said Mum. "He'll soon sort out a couple of dogs. He's probably bigger than they are, anyway!"

Chapter Two

By Saturday morning Mum had been to the pet shop and bought two collars and leads, two identity discs, two dog beds, two dog dishes, one water bowl, a big bag of Bonios, a cupboard full of dog tins, and a selection of rubber balls and squeaky toys. Susan sat and cuddled Oscar and whispered words of comfort in his ear.

"You must remember, Oscar, that dogs are *inferior*. And that you're number one, because you were here first."

She looked at Mum and Sally, stocking the shelves with dog tins.

"Honestly! Such a fuss they're making! Anyone would think they were expecting a new *baby* in the house."

Sally couldn't really see that there was all that much difference. Babies needed cots: dogs needed beds. Babies needed baby food: dogs needed dog food. And they both needed toys. They would get bored if they didn't have anything to play with.

She said so to Susan, but Susan just tossed her head.

"Oscar doesn't get bored. He's got more sense." She picked Oscar up under his armpits and rubbed her face against his. "He doesn't need silly stupid toys to play with, does he?"

Oscar purred loudly and agreed that he didn't.

"Oscar is a cat of *brain*," said Susan.

"He wasn't when he was young," said Mum. "He's had clockwork mice in his time."

"Yes," said Susan, "but now he prefers to sit and think. He doesn't want to be hassled by *dogs*!"

She draped Oscar over her shoulder and went huffing upstairs to her bedroom. Susan had obviously decided that she and Dad and

Oscar were going to form an alliance against Mum and Sally and the dogs. But unlike Susan, Dad was being helpful. He had been all round the garden and made the fence secure, blocking any holes and even putting up trellis.

"There we are!" said Dad, proud of his handiwork. "I reckon that'd keep a wolfhound in. Not," he added, hastily, "that we are having a wolfhound."

"Certainly not!" laughed Mum. "Just two little dear sweet mongrels."

Mum and Sally set off for Edenbridge immediately after breakfast. Mum was every bit as twittery as Sally.

"It *is* rather like adopting a baby," she said. "But you won't get too sad, Sally, will you? There are going to be lots and lots of dogs there and we can't take all of them."

"No, I know that," said Sally. "But other people will come and take them, won't they?"

"Oh, yes!" said Mum. "We won't be the only ones."

The entrance to End of the Road was down a long bumpy cart track over which the car bounced rather alarmingly. At any other time it would have made Sally feel sick, but today she was too excited. Mum parked the car in a small car park at the end of the track, by a notice which said "WELCOME TO END OF THE ROAD! Please take care to close the gate."

As soon as Sally opened the car door she could hear the sound of dogs barking. She followed Mum through the gate, making sure to close it behind her, and into a cobbled yard rather like a farmyard or a stables. All down one side of the yard were large pens, with wire mesh runs. Most of the pens had a couple of dogs in them, though some had three and just now and again there was a pen with only one. Almost all of the dogs were barking frantically, some of them actually hurling themselves against the wire in their eagerness to be noticed.

Mum took hold of Sally's hand.

"Let's go straight to the office."

Sally would have liked to stay and talk to some of the poor barking dogs, but Mum hustled her across the yard to a hut marked RECEPTION. There was quite a crowd of people in Reception, visitors like Mum and Sally. Sally felt a bit better when she saw that. Maybe the dogs only had to stay here a day or two before some kind person came and took them away.

The lady who ran the rescue centre was called Madge Warren. She was tall and slim, dressed in sweater and riding breeches. Sally decided there and then that when she was grown up she would run a rescue centre and look like Madge Warren.

Mum said, "I'm Jennifer Barnes. I spoke to you earlier in the week."

"Oh, yes! You've come to see the two little girls."

"That's right," said Mum. She squeezed Sally's hand. "This is my daughter, Sally. She's really been looking forward to this!"

"So's Mum," said Sally.

Madge Warren laughed.

"That's what I like to hear! Come and have a look. I'm sure you'll find them irresistible."

She led the way across the yard to the row of pens.

"Here we are! Minnie and Widget. That

one's Minnie." She pointed to a small black dog with a long chunky body and short bandy legs. "That one's Widget."

Widget was the same size as Minnie but sandy-coloured and not as chunky. She had big pobble eyes and white whiskers. Minnie had four white paws and a white blaze down her front.

"Don't ask me what they are," said Madge Warren, "because I really couldn't tell you. We think perhaps Minnie is half Dachshund and Widget possibly has a bit of whippet in her. They're lovely little people. We've had them for just over a month."

"They've been here a *month*?" said Sally.

"I won't let them be separated, you see; it's not right. They've been together since they were tiny pups."

"It wouldn't be kind," said Mum.

"No, it wouldn't. Dogs are capable of forming very close bonds. This is what some people don't realize. They seem to think that animals are just objects, like cars, to be sold on when you've got tired of them."

"Why were they brought in?" said Mum.

Madge Warren pulled a face.

"Owner had a new baby. Said she couldn't cope. Minnie in particular is supposed to be a handful."

Minnie at that moment was jumping up and down against the wire. She jumped so vigorously that she kept bouncing off it. Widget was standing on her hind legs, doing her best to lick fingers through the mesh. Widget was making little whiffling sounds, Minnie was barking. Sally knew exactly what they were saying. Minnie was saying, "Take me, take me, take me!" Widget was saying, "Please! Please! Please!" How could anyone bear to part with two such beautiful dogs?

"*Jumps on furniture.*" Madge Warren had removed a card from the frame on the front of the pen and was reading from it. "*Pulls on the lead. Chases cats.*"

"All quite normal doggy things," said Mum. "But she won't chase our cat more than once. He'll soon put her in her place!"

"Between you and me," said Madge Warren, "I think the woman just wanted to get rid of them. Oh, you'd be surprised!"

she said, as Sally's mouth opened in protest. "The number of people who have animals and then decide they can't be bothered with them."

"We can be bothered," said Sally, trying to stroke Widget through the netting.

"A dog is for life," said Mum.

"We've got a sticker in the back of our car." Sally announced it, proudly. "*A dog is for life, not just for Christmas.*"

"You sound as if you'd be the perfect owners. Why don't you try taking them for a trot round the ring, see how you get on?"

"We'll get on," said Mum; but Madge Warren insisted.

"It will give you time to make up your mind."

Sally's mind was already made up, and she knew that Mum's was, too. If she and Mum were the perfect owners, then Minnie and Widget were the perfect dogs!

"I'll go and get them out for you."

Madge Warren disappeared round the back of the row of pens, reappearing seconds later with Minnie and Widget on their leads.

"Just a few turns round the ring ... get to know one another."

Mum took Minnie, because she was the stronger of the two, and Sally took Widget. It was true that Minnie did pull, rather, but as Mum said, she was excited – and probably hadn't had much exercise for the past month.

"She'll learn!"

"And anyway," said Sally, "when they're in the park they won't need to be on the lead."

"We'll take a ball. That will soon get the wind out of their tails." Mum giggled, happily. "They're funny-looking little things, aren't they? Wouldn't win any prizes at Cruft's!"

Sally supposed they were a bit funny, Minnie with her short legs and Widget with her pobble eyes, but that was all right. Sally herself was rather a funny little thing. Her best friend Gemma had once kindly informed her that she had a face like a bun.

"A big squidgy bun."

It was true that Sally had told Gemma she had sticking-out teeth and ears that flapped in the breeze. They quite often insulted each other; it was all part of being best friends. Gemma had also said that Sally had frog's eyes.

"All big and poppy ... but your hair is quite nice."

Sally's hair was thick and black and shiny, like Minnie's. She wore it cut in a fringe and curling round her ears.

"Just a pity about the nose," sighed Gemma. "More like a blob than a nose."

Widget had a bloblike nose. She also had great big bloblike feet at the end of funny little matchstick legs. Nobody would give her any prizes for beauty. But you couldn't help the way you were born.

"Mum!" Sally said it anxiously. "We are going to take them, aren't we?"

"I wouldn't part with them for the world!" said Mum. "Let's go back and do the necessary."

While Mum and Minnie stayed in Reception, with Mum filling out forms and making a donation, Sally wandered off with Widget to look at all the other dogs. She knew they couldn't rescue any more; she was only going to look.

By now there were several families in the yard, all in search of a dog to adopt. The dogs were going frantic, scrabbling for attention. As she and Widget walked past the row of pens, Sally heard a girl of about her own age say, "Mum! This one! Can we have this one?" Then she heard a man talking to a woman: "How about this chap here? He looks as if he'd do us."

Sally was filled with a deep sense of contentment: all the dogs were going to be adopted! She didn't need to worry about them.

Only one cage didn't have any people round it. It was a small cage right at the end, tacked on to the others almost as an after-thought. An old dog was lying there, slumped into the corner with its head between its paws. Sally could tell that it was old because its muzzle was as grey as her gran's hair. Its coat was a mixture of black and white, with tan feathers on the back legs and a long bushy tail. Sally knew that it was a border collie, the sort that farmers use for herding sheep.

"Hallo, doggie!" Sally crouched down,

sticking the tips of her fingers through the wire mesh of the cage and waggling them. The old dog continued to lie there, head between paws, not moving.

"Are you all right?" said Sally. She waggled her fingers again. "Poor doggie! Don't look so sad. Someone will come and rescue you soon."

But nobody seemed interested in the old black and white collie slumped in its corner. Not even Widget seemed interested. All Widget wanted to do was lick. Lick lap lick, went her tongue over Sally's face. Sally giggled and pushed her away.

"Stop it!" she said. "Talk to this poor doggie."

From somewhere in the yard a woman's voice called "Beth!" The old dog lifted its head.

"*Beth!*" called the woman.

At first Sally thought that she was calling the dog, but then she called again, "Beth, will you come along? We're going," and she knew that it was a mother calling her child.

"Beth?" Sally said it softly. The old dog

turned to look at her. "Beth? Beth? Come here, Beth!"

Slowly, the old dog moved the tip of her tail.

"Come on, Beth! Come!"

But Beth wouldn't. Instead, with a sigh, she let her head slump back between her paws. It was as if she was saying, "Beth is my name, but you are not my owner."

"Sal?" Mum had come to fetch her, with Minnie throttling herself on the end of the lead. "We've done everything, we can go now."

"Oh, Mum, look!" Sally plucked at Mum's arm. "Look at this poor old dog!"

"Yes, we're rather worried about her." Madge Warren had come over. She stood, absently fondling Widget. "She's pining terribly. Doesn't respond at all. And at her age she's never going to find another home for herself."

Sally turned a distressed face towards her. "Why not?"

"Too old," said Madge Warren. "Nobody wants an old dog. We think she must be at least fourteen. We don't actually know because we don't know anything about her. She was left here just over a fortnight ago."

"Left?" said Mum.

"Yes, we found her one morning, tied to the gatepost, with twenty pounds in an envelope and a note asking us to look after her. I'm afraid we're not making a very good job of it, are we, old girl?"

Madge Warren bent down and clicked her fingers. The old dog didn't even lift her head.

"What —" Sally's lower lip had begun to quiver — "what will happen to her? If nobody takes her?"

Madge Warren didn't reply; simply shrugged her shoulders and turned down the corners of her mouth. The tears started to Sally's eyes. Susan was always jeering at her, telling her she was a crybaby. She did cry quite easily; but surely anyone would cry at the thought of a poor old dog whom nobody wanted? Even Mum was biting her lips. Mum was a bit like Sally. They had wept buckets together over *Black Beauty* and *Lassie Come Home* when they saw them on television. Dad said they were a couple of old softies.

"Mum!" begged Sally. "Mum, couldn't we –"

"Oh, Sally! Darling. Be sensible! How could we? Your dad would have a fit."

"He wouldn't, Mum! He wouldn't! He said ... I don't care how many dogs you have!"

Mum was wavering, she could tell.

"He said we could have a dozen, if that's what you wanted!"

"I don't think he really meant it," murmured Mum.

"If he didn't mean it, he shouldn't have said it! Oh, Mum, please!"

Mum flicked a glance at Madge Warren.

"Would you advise it?"

Madge Warren spread her hands.

"You put me in a difficult position. I'd love nothing better than for someone to give the old girl a home. But I have to be honest. She's not eating properly. Nobody's been able to get through to her. We don't even know her name."

"I know her name!" Sally squatted by the side of the cage. "It's Beth!"

The old dog didn't open her eyes, but slowly the tip of her tail moved.

"See?" Sally looked up at her mum in triumph. "She's called Beth!"

"Well, that is pretty remarkable," said Madge Warren, "I must say. That's the first time I've seen even a glimmer of response."

"Mum?"

"Sally, love, I really don't think—"

"*Mum!*" Sally cried it in anguish. "We can't just go away and leave her here!"

"Darling, listen." Mum crouched at Sally's side. "Be realistic. I know how you feel, but she's an old dog – a very old dog. She's not going to live that much longer. You'd just be starting to get fond of her and it would be time to say goodbye."

Sally scrubbed, rather fiercely, at her eyes.

"I wouldn't mind!"

"You would," said Mum. "We both would. It would be terribly distressing."

"You're just thinking of us!" accused Sally. "I'm thinking of Beth!"

The old dog's tail thumped on the floor of the cage.

"That certainly appears to be her name," said Madge Warren. "But whether, at her time of life, she could ever learn to bond with new people – I don't know!" She shook her head. "I have to say, I somehow doubt it."

"She could!" said Sally. "She's already starting to know me. Watch when I call! Beth? Beth? Come here, Beth! Say hallo to me!"

Please, Beth ... please do it!

Slowly, Beth raised her old grey head and slid her eyes in Sally's direction. One of them looked cloudy, like skimmed milk.

"Cataract," muttered Madge Warren. Mum nodded. All three of them held their breath.

"Beth?" whispered Sally.

With a deep sigh, Beth hauled herself to her feet and stiffly padded her way across the cage. Sally turned, with shining eyes, to her mum and Madge Warren.

"You see?" she said. "You see?"

"It looks," said Mum, in rather a shaky voice, "as if we've just acquired another dog..."

On the way home in the car, Sally sat in the

back of the car with Minnie and Widget on one side and Beth on the other. Minnie and Widget were excited. Minnie kept barking and Widget kept whiffling as they glued their noses to the windows, trying to catch the scents of the outside world. Beth lay quietly, with her head on Sally's lap.

"She's really happy," said Sally. "She's really grateful to us for taking her."

Mum glanced back at her in the driving mirror.

"I dread to think what your dad's going to say."

"He can't say anything," said Sally. "He told us ... we could have a dozen if we wanted. Anyway –" she placed an arm protectively over Beth's shoulders – "we're not giving her back, whatever he says. She's our dog, now!"

Chapter Three

Dad's eyes nearly fell out of his head when he saw how many dogs Mum and Sally had come back with.

"What's this?" he said.

"Oh, Dad!" wailed Sally.

"Oh, Alistair!" pleaded Mum.

"She was ever so unhappy, Dad!"

"Honestly, Ali, if you'd seen her –"

"We *had* to bring her, Dad."

"It was heartbreaking. Truly!"

"She was left there, Dad. Tied to a gatepost. People are so *foul*."

"They are," said Mum. "They're disgusting. A poor old dog of that age –"

"It's *cruel*," said Sally.

There was a silence. Beth lay at Sally's feet, pressed hard up against her. (Minnie and Widget had gone racing off to explore the back garden.) Beth looked at Dad; Dad looked at Beth. Dad saw an old grey dog with a thinning coat and a cloudy eye. Beth, perhaps, didn't see very much at all. Madge Warren had said she wasn't sure how much sight she had left in either eye.

"Very little, I fear. But loss of sight doesn't matter so much to a dog as it does to a person. They have their other senses. You'd be surprised how well they cope."

"Dad?" said Sally.

Dad shook his head.

"I dunno," he said. "You can't be trusted, can you? Either of you! Your mum's as bad as you are. In fact I'm not sure she isn't worse."

"It wasn't Mum's fault," said Sally. She twisted her fingers in Beth's ruff. Beth's tail slowly thumped. "I was the one who wanted her."

"In that case, you'd better be the one who looks after her."

"I will," said Sally. "I promise!"

"Oh, Ali, you are so good!" said Mum.

"I know I am," said Dad. "I'm going off to buy myself a load more tools this afternoon."

"That's right," said Mum. "Power drills and fretsaws and – and just whatever you've always wanted!"

Susan came home at lunch time carrying shopping bags full of junk. She always bought junk when she went into town. Beads and bangles, pairs of tights (she already had about six thousand), tubes of lipstick, pots of eye paint, bottles of nail varnish. Total rubbish if you asked Sally, but she had to make herself look beautiful for spotty old Justin.

Susan's jaw fell open when she saw all the dogs.

"*Three?*" she shrieked. "Where's Oscar?"

Oscar was sitting on top of the fridge.

"He's already bashed Minnie and Widget," said Sally. "But he didn't use his claws. He just bopped them one and now they respect him."

He hadn't had to bop Beth because she didn't annoy him as the younger ones did. Sally thought that Oscar quite liked Beth. He had crept up to her as she lay there and cautiously sniffed her all over, from the top of her head to the tip of her tail. He had then retreated to the fridge, where he had conducted a vigorous washing session. Now he sat on his elbows, coolly surveying the scene.

"You don't have to worry about Oscar," said Mum.

"But you must be *mad*." Susan's eyes roved the kitchen, from Minnie and Widget playing tug of war with a length of knotted rope, to Beth lying quietly in her corner. "They're not so bad." She nodded at the two little ones. "But what on earth did you want to go and get that one for?"

"She's mine!" Sally flew across the kitchen and hurled herself down at Beth's side. "She's a good dog! She let Oscar sniff her."

"She's old," said Susan. "She's practically decrepit."

"Old dogs have just as much right to be loved and cared for as young ones," said Mum. "Oscar will be old and decrepit one day. What do you suggest we do then? Throw him out?"

"That's different!" Susan hoisted Oscar down from the fridge and cradled him in her arms. "Oscar's ours."

"So's Beth, now," said Sally.

"It's not the same! It's all right when it's your own pet. You don't mind them getting a bit grungy and smelly."

"Beth isn't grungy and smelly!"

"She will be," said Susan. "Her breath'll start stinking and she'll make messes everywhere."

"Oh, be quiet!" cried Sally.

"Susan is right in a way," said Mum. "It takes a very special sort of person to bring an old dog into their home and love it. It's not something that just anybody could do. But imagine, for instance, if Oscar were old and something terrible happened which meant that he was left on his own ... wouldn't you like to think that there was someone, somewhere, like Sally, who was prepared to give him a home?"

"Oh, I suppose so." Susan dumped Oscar on a chair and flounced across to the sink. She hated anyone to get the better of her. "But you wait till she has to start clearing up the messes . . . I bet she won't be quite so fond of it then!"

"I will!" Sally put her face close to Beth's. "I'll always love you, whatever happens."

After lunch, Dad went off to the DIY to moon about amongst the tools while Mum and Sally prepared to take the dogs up to the park for a run. Grudgingly, at the last minute, Susan announced that she would come with them.

"You don't have to," said Sally.

"I know I don't *have* to."

Sally would just as soon have been on her own with Mum. Susan was going through what Mum called "an awkward phase", which meant that she held both Mum and Sally in total contempt. Whatever they said was wrong; whatever they did was ridiculous.

"I thought you didn't like dogs?" said Sally.

"I never said I didn't like dogs! When did I say I didn't like dogs?"

"You s—"

"Oh, girls, please!" begged Mum. "Let's just enjoy the walk."

"Dunno how far you think that one's going to go," said Susan, jerking her head at Beth.

"We'll see how she does," said Mum.

Beth walked slowly, always keeping close to Sally. It was as if she had made up her mind she was Sally's dog. She moved a little stiffly, limping slightly on her right back leg, but she took a proper doggy interest in what was going on around her, pausing every now and again to investigate a smell or nose about amongst the bushes. Mum said that was good.

"It shows she's enjoying herself."

The two little ones were like jumping jacks, running, bouncing, barking. Minnie ran with her ears a-flap, yards of pink tongue lolling from her mouth, long body looping, cater-pillar-like. Widget was faster and more nimble, flying fairy fashion across the grass on her dainty legs with the big pobble feet.

Susan laughed. "They're brilliant, those two!"

Sally's heart swelled. She was glad that Susan approved of Minnie and Widget, but what about Beth? She was just as brilliant, in her own way. You couldn't expect an old dog to run and jump and spring about like puppies. Old dogs had other qualities. Old dogs were ... *special*. That was what they were. Gentle and special and in need of lots of love.

On their way back, through an avenue of trees where squirrels were busy hoarding nuts for winter, and Minnie and Widget were busy trying to round them up, they heard, in the distance, someone whistling a dog. Two short notes, like the notes of the cuckoo. Beth must have heard them, too, for she suddenly stopped and froze, ears pricked, head to one side, listening.

The whistle came again, the same two notes. Beth looked at Sally and made a little apologetic whimpering sound. The whimper seemed to say, "I'm sorry, but I have to go now!"

Beth turned, and started loping off through the trees, back the way they had come.

"Beth?" called Sally.

The whistle came again; and then a man appeared, walking briskly, with a red setter at his heels.

Beth stopped. Her head drooped, her tail went down.

"Beth!" Sally ran to her. The old dog turned. She seemed sad and puzzled. What had she been expecting?

The man with the red setter nodded.

"Afternoon," he said.

Mum and Susan said good afternoon back to him.

"Beautiful day," said Mum.

"Beautiful!" said the man.

The man and the red setter went on their way. Sally walked slowly back, up the avenue, with Beth at her side.

"Well," said Mum. "She's shown she can move if she wants to – and her hearing is obviously still acute."

"But what did she think it was?" wondered Sally.

It was Susan who came up with the suggestion that maybe her previous owner had whistled her like that.

"She probably thought she'd found them again."

The ready tears sprang to Sally's eyes.

"Oh, Beth! Poor Beth!"

For once Susan didn't jeer or call her a crybaby. Gruffly she said, "She's all right now. She's got you."

"But she still feels unhappy!" wept Sally.

"I'm sure she won't for long," said Mum. "She's taken to you in a big way. She's already following you around like a shadow!"

Dad came home at tea time with something he said he had always wanted: a real tool chest to put his tools in.

"Isn't that nice?" said Mum. "You've got your tool chest, we've got our dogs."

"What have I got?" said Susan.

"You've got Oscar," said Sally.

"I've always had Oscar," said Susan; but she didn't sound too disgruntled.

After tea, Dad rushed out to the shed to put his tools away in their new tool chest, Susan went upstairs to have a bath and make herself look beautiful for going out with spotty Justin, and Sally wandered off down the garden with the dogs. They found Oscar hard asleep in a nest of leaves beneath a flowering currant bush. He opened one eye as Minnie and

Widget ran barking towards him, but they had learnt their lesson. One bop was enough: you don't mess with a cat like Oscar!

Sally sat in the garden for perhaps twenty minutes, throwing a ball for the two little ones, with Oscar curled nose to tail in his nest of leaves and Beth stretched out beside him.

Sally said, "Good *girl*, Beth! Good *boy*, Oscar!"

She wished that Susan could see them, old dog and big ginger tom, lying there together.

She became aware that Minnie and Widget were grizzling: their ball had disappeared into a tangled mess of bushes near Dad's tool shed.

"I'll get it," said Sally. "You two stay there," she told Beth and Oscar; but Beth and Oscar had no intention of moving. It was a warm October evening, and they were comfortable.

Sally ran down the garden, Minnie and Widget banging and bumping at her side. As she scrabbled in the undergrowth, searching for the ball, she heard Mum's voice coming from the tool shed.

"You don't seriously mind, do you, Ali?"

And then her dad's voice: "I told you, sweetheart ... anything that makes you happy."

And Mum said, "Oh, Ali!" in a sloppy kind of way, and there was a bit of silence, during which Sally found the ball and tossed it up the garden and the two dogs went bowling after it.

Sally was about to scrabble back out of the undergrowth when she heard her dad's voice again.

"Mind you, I hope you realize that it's going to cost a small fortune putting three dogs in a kennel when we go off on holiday."

Put them in a kennel? Sally was indignant. She wasn't putting Beth in any kennel! It would be a terrible thing to do. Beth would think she was being abandoned again. Sally would rather not have a holiday if it meant leaving Beth behind.

To her relief she heard her mum's voice, light and laughing: "We'll get a cottage somewhere and take them with us!"

"Three dogs and four people all packed into one small car? Be practical, Jen!"

"So we'll buy ourselves an estate."

"I only wish we could."

Then there was another bit of silence and her mum's voice spoke again, but not laughing, this time. Quite grave and sombre.

"To be perfectly honest, Ali, I doubt there'll be three of them by then. The collie's extremely old. They said at the kennels she's not eating properly. She's not going to last all that long."

Sally caught her breath. How could Mum say such a thing? Dogs could live to be sixteen! They could live to be seventeen. They could live to be eighteen!

She heard her dad's voice, equally grave: "Do you think, in the circumstances, it was quite wise to let Sally have her?"

And her mum said, "Probably not, but she wanted her so."

"It'll all end in tears," said Dad.

Sally turned and went galloping back to the end of the garden. She didn't want to hear any more. She wished she'd never listened. Grown-ups were hateful!

At six o'clock Mum prepared food for the animals. Oscar had his on top of the fridge, where the dogs couldn't interfere with him. Minnie and Widget had theirs side by side near the back door, served in their brand new dog bowls. There wasn't a dog bowl for Beth so Mum sacrificed one of her special oven-proof dishes.

"There you are," she said. "Brown rice and chicken, and lots of vitamin pills." Mum handed the dish to Sally. "You give it to her. She's your dog."

Beth didn't seem very interested when Sally put the dish before her. She took one look at it and turned away.

"Mum!" wailed Sally. "She's not eating!"

Mum and Dad exchanged glances.

"Try coaxing her," said Mum.

Sally murmured and pleaded. She heaped chicken and rice on to a spoon and pretended to eat it herself.

"Mm! Yummy yummy! I'm enjoying it!"

Beth just lay, with her head on her paws. It wasn't until Sally dolloped the contents of the spoon into her hand and held it out to her that at last her nose began to twitch and she agreed to have a tiny taste.

"Good girl!" crooned Sally. "Good girl!"

Little by little, feeding out of Sally's hand, Beth cleared the plate. It took her a long time, but she did it. Sally was jubilant.

"Mum! She's eaten the lot!"

"Talk about spoon feeding," sniffed Susan, who had appeared in the kitchen in time to see Sally scooping up the last handful.

"She needs to build her strength up," said Sally. "So long as she's eating she'll be all right, won't she, Mum?"

"It's certainly an encouraging sign," said Mum.

When Sally went to bed that night, Beth tried to go with her. At first Mum said no, because it was one of the rules that Dad had made: no dogs in bedrooms. But she whimpered so, at the foot of the stairs, that in the end even Dad's heart was softened.

"All right," he said. "I'll make an exception for this one, because she's old. But you two —" he looked sternly at Minnie and Widget, sitting together like a pair of little bookends — "you stay in the kitchen, in your baskets. And Sally!" he called, as Beth and Sally padded together up the stairs. "I don't want her sleeping in your bed, right? She stays on the floor."

"Yes, Dad."

There was a large fluffy rug on Sally's floor. Sally pulled it over to the bed and Beth obediently settled herself, for all the world as if she had understood what Dad had said. Maybe she had. Sally had read in the dog book that border collies were the intellectuals of the canine world. Minnie and Widget were fun, but they were silly skittering little things compared with Sally's beautiful Beth. She remembered what Mum had said to Dad in the garden shed, and frosty fingers crept up her spine and made her shiver. She slipped out of bed and snuggled close to Beth on the rug.

"Please, Beth," she whispered, "stay with us for a long time . . . for a long long *long* time, Beth!"

Chapter Four

Some time during the night – it turned out, when she looked at her bedside clock, to be exactly midnight – Sally was woken by the sound of gentle whimpering. She opened her eyes to find Beth standing with her front paws on the edge of the bed, her face next to Sally's. Sally switched on the light.

"Beth," she whispered. "What's the matter?"

Beth's tail waved slowly to and fro. There didn't seem to be anything the matter.

"What do you want?" whispered Sally.

It was obvious what she wanted: she wanted to get into bed.

"You're not allowed," said Sally; but Beth

just laid her head on the pillow, gazing up at Sally with all the love and longing she was capable of. She couldn't have asked more plainly if she had had words to speak with.

"I don't know what Dad will say if he finds out," said Sally.

She pulled back the duvet and Beth scrambled up. In spite of old age and stiffness, she could just about make it. When she was young, she must have been a champion jumper. Sally pictured her flying over hedges and ditches, over streams and fences and five-barred gates. Nothing would have stopped her!

"I wish I'd known you when you were young," whispered Sally.

Beth snuggled down beneath the duvet with a sigh of deep contentment. She stayed there till six o'clock in the morning. At six o'clock she slipped back out on to her rug, and when Dad came in an hour later with a cup of tea (Dad always brought tea on a Sunday) she opened an eye and yawned and stretched like a dog who had been lying there all night long. Sally thought that was really clever of her –

but then, as the dog book said, border collies were the intellectuals of the canine world.

"How did she sleep?" Mum asked Sally, as Sally and Beth came down to breakfast.

"She slept really well," said Sally.

"That's good. I thought she might get you up in the night ... dogs of that age can't always hold themselves."

"Which is why," said Dad, "she ought to be down in the kitchen."

"Oh, Dad!" wailed Sally. "You promised!"

"What did I promise?"

"You said she could sleep in my room!"

"So long as she doesn't get into the bed."

Sally was quiet a moment, pressing the back of her spoon against her shredded wheat so that the milk could get in. She didn't like shredded wheat when it was hard; she preferred it soft and mushy. Susan accused her of eating pap.

"Like a baby!"

"We'll have no dogs in beds and no dogs on furniture," said Dad.

"Why can't they?" said Sally.

Dad wasn't the sort of person to say,

"Because I tell you so." He always gave a reason.

"A) because we don't want hairs over everything and B) because it's not healthy."

"In olden days dogs always used to sleep with people ... they slept together on the floor." Sally had read about it in books. "They had huge big halls and they slept on straw."

"Yes, and they died of hideous diseases. Ever heard of the plague?"

"That was rats," said Sally.

"It was fleas!"

"*Rat* fleas. Not dog."

"You'd still get hair," said Susan. "I don't want dog hair all over my clothes, thank you very much."

"I don't see why not! You already have cat hair. Nobody stops Oscar getting on the furniture."

"It's very difficult to discipline cats," said Mum.

"Cats have more brain," said Susan.

"They do not! Mum, it's not fair!"

"No, I suppose it isn't," agreed Mum. "Not when you stop to think about it." She shot a sideways glance at Dad.

"We are *not*," said Dad, "having dogs on the furniture. Nor," he added, "in the beds."

It wasn't very often that Dad put his foot down, but when he did Mum never argued.

"Dad isn't really an animal person," she said, as she and Sally, with the three dogs on the lead, set out for the park. "We mustn't push him too hard. He's been very good."

"Would you mind dogs on the furniture?" said Sally.

"Me?" Mum laughed. "You know me! I'm an old softie. I wouldn't mind where they went."

"Even in bed?" said Sally.

"We-e-e-ll..." Mum paused to untangle Minnie's lead from Widget's. "I must admit that my old Beardie used to sleep with me every night, but I expect it probably wasn't such a good thing, really."

"Why not? Why wasn't it?"

"Oh! I don't know," said Mum. "It prob-ably wasn't very hygienic."

Sally knew that Mum didn't really believe it; she wouldn't mind Beth sleeping in the bed. It was just Dad, because he wasn't an animal person.

"We're really very lucky," said Mum. "There are some husbands who wouldn't let their wives have three dogs."

"Do wives always have to do what husbands say?"

"No! Of course they don't. But when people are married they have to try not to do things which upset each other. So if one person feels very strongly *against* something, it's usually wisest for the other person to give in."

Sally tossed her hair back.

"I shan't give in! When I get married I'm going to marry an animal person. Then I can have just as many dogs as I like. I'll probably have at least a dozen. And cats, as well."

"In that case," said Mum, "you'd better make sure you do marry an animal person!"

They walked from one end of the park to the other, right down as far as the avenue of trees. They met the man with the red setter again, but this time he wasn't whistling. The red setter was called Fergus.

"He seems to have taken a real shine to your collie," said Fergus's owner.

"He obviously goes for the older woman," said Mum.

Mum and Fergus's owner laughed. Sally couldn't see anything particularly funny about it.

"He goes for her because she's beautiful," she said to Mum, as they walked on.

"She's a lovely lacy lady," said Mum. "All got up in her frills and furbelows... I must take her in to the vet tomorrow and get that back leg looked at."

"It won't be anything serious, Mum, will it?"

"Just a touch of arthritis, I should think. I'll ask him to check her heart while I'm there."

"Her heart?" Sally's own heart missed a beat. "Why do you want him to do that?"

"Not because I think there's anything wrong. Don't start panicking! It's just that it's always sensible, with an old dog. I want to make sure everything's in order."

After lunch, Gemma came round. Sally

hadn't told her about her and Mum not being able to be trusted and coming home with what Dad referred to as "a pack". She was surprised to find the kitchen full of dogs.

"Oh, it's not fair!" she squealed. "I'm not even allowed to have one!"

"You can share ours," said Sally. "But you'd better make a fuss of Oscar first, or he'll feel left out. It's like having a new baby in the house ... you have to pay extra special attention to the one that was here first or they get jealous. Susan got *really* jealous when I was born."

Oscar didn't show any signs of being jealous or feeling left out, but Gemma obediently cuddled him and assured him that he was still number one.

"Bees' knees in the world," said Gemma.

Sally giggled. "What's that mean?"

"Means he's the best," said Gemma. But Oscar already knew that!

With Oscar happily settled on his fridge eating cat biscuits, Sally and Gemma went into the garden with the dogs.

"These two are so *sweet*," crooned Gemma,

as Minnie chased Widget and Widget chased her tail.

"Showing off," said Sally. "They do it all the time." She picked up a ball and threw it. Minnie and Widget instantly went streaming off, down the garden.

"What about that one?" Gemma nodded at Beth, lying in her favourite spot, under the flowering currant. "Why doesn't she play?"

"She's too old," said Sally. "She's about fourteen."

"What did you want an old one for? Why didn't you get another young one? I suppose she was all they had left."

"She was not!" Sally rose up in fury. "I *chose* her."

"But she can't do anything!"

"So what?"

"Well, but I mean…" Gemma faltered. "She's kind of a bit … grotty. Isn't she?"

"She's not grotty! That's a hateful thing to say! How'd you like it if someone said your nan was a bit grotty? Just because she's old!"

"Sorry." Gemma backed off, hastily. "I'm sorry!"

"If you want to know," said Sally, "I chose her because she was sad. Because she'd been abandoned. *I* don't care if she can't play games! She still needs someone to love her."

Gemma knelt contritely at Beth's side.

"She must have been really beautiful when she was young."

"She still is!" Sally said it fiercely. "There's a red setter goes in the park who's her boyfriend. Mum says she's like a lovely lacy lady."

"Mm." Gemma nodded. "All the frilly bits."

"They're called feathers, those bits on her legs. And she's a tri-colour 'cause she's not just black and white but black and white and tan. That's special. You don't get many tri-colours."

"Why was she abandoned?"

"Nobody knows," said Sally. "But whoever owned her must have been *foul*."

"Yes," said Gemma. "They must have been. *Absolutely* foul."

Sally really hated having to go to school on Monday and leave Beth behind.

"She'll still be here when you get back," said Mum. "Don't worry!"

Sally couldn't help worrying, just a little bit; not because she was leaving Beth behind but because Mum was taking her to the vet.

"He's going to look at her back leg," she said to Gemma. "And check her heart."

Susan, at breakfast, trying for once to be kind, had said, "Let's face it, if there's anything wrong it's best to find out now, before you've had a chance to grow fond of her."

Gemma knew better than to say such a thing. She knew that Sally had already grown fond of her.

"I bet she'll be OK," she said. "My nan had to go for heart tests last week – my *old* nan – and they said she was A1. And my nan," said Gemma, "is seventy-three!"

It wasn't all that much of a comfort. Mum had said that to find out how old a dog was in human terms you had to multiply its age by seven. Seven times fourteen made Beth ninety-eight. Ninety-eight was *really* old. Ninety-eight was ancient. But at least Gemma understood how Sally felt, which was more than Susan did.

When Miss Carpenter, in class, accused Sally of not paying attention, it was Gemma who said, "She's worried about her dog, Miss." And then of course Miss Carpenter wanted to know why, and Sally had to tell her (and all the rest of the class) about finding Beth at the rescue centre, and how she had been abandoned, and how Mum was taking her to the vet.

Miss Carpenter said, "Tomorrow you must let us know how she is. But I shouldn't think the rescue centre would have let her be re-homed if they thought there was anything seriously wrong with her."

That cheered Sally up slightly and made her feel a bit braver. All the same, she could hardly wait for going-home time.

When the 3.30 bell rang, Sally was first out into the playground. Mum was waiting for her as usual, by the gates. She had Beth on the lead. Beth wagged and wagged when she saw Sally.

"Oh, she's your dog all right!" said Mum.

"I brought her with me because I thought you'd like to take her for a quick walk round the park. She's been checked out and her heart is fine. She's just got a slight touch of arthritis in her back leg, so I've splashed out and got her some evening primrose capsules. But whatever you do," said Mum, "don't tell your dad!"

Cheekily, all fears forgotten, Sally said, "Why? Wouldn't he like it?"

"He'd say, 'Evening *primrose*? For a *dog*?'"

"Like that time you got special cat milk for Oscar!"

"Your dad doesn't understand," said Mum, "that to people like you and me, animals are just as important as human beings."

That evening, while they were watching television, Beth tried to smuggle herself up on to the sofa beside Sally. Dad said, "Sally! Get that dog off the furniture."

"Dad, she's old!" said Sally. "She needs somewhere comfortable. Sh—"

"You heard what I said," said Dad.

Sally spent the rest of the evening defiantly

sitting on the floor. If Beth couldn't be with her, then she would be with Beth. Dad just didn't understand about animals.

On the stroke of midnight, Beth climbed into Sally's bed again; on the very dot of six, she slipped out.

"You are such an intelligent girl!" whispered Sally.

Next day at school, everyone wanted to know what had happened at the vet. Sally told them, and Miss Carpenter said, "That's excellent news! She's a very lucky dog, having people like you and your mum to look after her."

And then she said, "You ought to go in for the Pets' Poetry competition! Have you heard about it? It was in the local paper. Do you take the local paper? Have a look when you go home this afternoon. It sounds right up your street."

Mum and Sally looked through the paper together. It was Mum who found the piece about the poetry competition.

"Oh, yes! Here we are ... *Local pet food manufacturers, Top Tins, are offering prizes for* the best poems written on the subject of *My Cat* or *My Dog*. There are three categories, Under-8, 9–11, and 12 +. First prize in each category will be a £20 voucher to be spent in any local pet shop and £50 worth of Top Tins. Entries to be received by 30 November. Winners will be announced in December.

"Well! It's worth a go," said Mum.

"I could write a poem about Oscar," said Susan.

"You could both write poems," said Mum. "You'd be in different categories, so you wouldn't clash."

Sally was lying in bed that night, trying to think of her first line – *My dog Beth is a border collie. I have a collie whose name is Beth* – when there was a tap at the door and her dad's head appeared. He saw Beth curled up on the rug and nodded.

"Good!" he said. "That's good. I thought for a moment I was going to find you lying on the floor with her."

Dad came over and sat on the edge of Sally's bed.

"Sal, I hope you're not going to become too

attached to this old thing." He pulled at the fur of Beth's ruff. "It can only end in tears, you know."

It was what he had said to Mum, when she had heard them talking in the shed.

"Dad, I do *know*." Sally said it earnestly. "But people shouldn't just throw out their old dogs as if they're rubbish. And if they do, then someone like me has to look after them."

"Look after her, by all means," said Dad. "Just don't get too attached." He dropped a kiss on Sally's forehead. "OK?"

The minute Dad left the room, Sally held up one corner of the duvet and Beth came scrambling in. An old dog needed a bed to sleep in; the floor was too hard, even with a rug. Dad ought to know that. He was always complaining about old bones, and he was only forty-six.

Sally fell asleep still trying to think of the first line of her poem.

I have a dog and her name is Beth...

It wasn't any use saying don't become too attached to her. Sally had lost her heart the

minute she had whispered the name "Beth"
and Beth had responded.

Beth is the name of my border collie...
I rescued a dog
Whose name was Beth...
"I love you, Beth!"
Beth's tail thumped, beneath the duvet.
"We'll win first prize," vowed Sally.
"That's what we'll do!"

Chapter Five

"**M**y Dog Beth."

Sally cleared her throat, importantly. Mum and Dad sat waiting. Susan said, "Why didn't you write about Widget and Min? You could have described them playing with their rope. They're really funny when they do that!"

Minnie and Widget played for hours with their bit of rope, chasing, tugging, growling, shaking. Sally agreed that they were funny, but Minnie and Widget were Mum's dogs.

"Beth is *mine*," she said. And Beth was special.

Susan humped a shoulder.

"Go on, then! Get on with it. What are we waiting for?"

"For the audience to be quiet," said Dad. "Come on, Sal! We're all ears."

Sally took up her poetry-reading position, feet neatly turned out like those of a ballet dancer.

"My Dog Beth.

"My dog Beth is a border collie,
  Black and white and tan.
  She's a lady dressed in lace
  And I'm her number one fan!

"She sleeps in my room
  On a rug by the bed,
  As good as gold can be.
  We lie there together
  The whole night through,
  My border collie and me.

"We go for walks in the park up the road
  And Beth has a boyfriend there.
  The boyfriend's name is Fergus O'Dowd,
  A setter with bright red hair.

"Fergus is young and handsome
While Beth is quite an old dog.
But that doesn't matter to Fergus,
He still admires her a lot!

"We love each other, my collie and me.
Right from the start, we both knew.
When Beth said 'Please!' and I said
    'Please!'
And Mum said, 'What can we do?'

"She was left at a rescue centre,
Tied outside to a gate.
Poor old dog, just left there!
Told to stay and wait.

"She looked so sad when we found her,
All by herself in a cage.
They said that no one would want her.
Who'd take a dog of that age?

"She never wagged, she hadn't eaten,
Never moved or made a sound.
Just lay like a dog that's been beaten,
With her head flat out on the ground.

"Even my mum was doubtful.
She said, 'Do you think that it's wise?'
But I called Beth's name and she wagged
   at me,
Then she raised her head
And I looked in her eyes
And I knew that it had to be.

"So we brought her home that very same
   day
And my dad said 'Oh!' and my sister said
   'No!'
But I said 'Yes,' and Mum did, too.
And now we're happy as happy can be,
My beautiful lacy lady and me!"

After Sally had finished, there was a long
silence.

"Is that all right, do you think?" said Sally.

"It's wonderful!" Sally couldn't decide
whether Mum was laughing or crying, or
maybe doing both together. Mum pulled out
her handkerchief and blotted at her eyes.
"Absolutely wonderful!"

"Very touching," said Dad. He blew his

nose. "I'm glad you didn't cast me as the villain!"

Sally was puzzled.

"What villain?" She hadn't put a villain in the poem.

"*And my dad said 'Oh!' and my sister said 'No!'*"

"I never!" said Susan. "I just said they were mad."

"Mad wouldn't have rhymed." Sally explained it patiently. She wasn't sure how much Susan understood about poetry. "I suppose I could have said 'My dad said "Bad!" and my sister said "Mad!"' But Dad didn't say bad, and anyway it sounds peculiar."

"That's right, so I have to get the blame," said Susan.

"It's only a poem," said Mum.

"I don't think it scans properly."

Susan made a grab for it; Sally snatched it back.

"It does!" She'd bounced the rhythm on her fingers, the way Miss Carpenter had taught them:

My dog BETH is a BORder COLLie
BLACK and WHITE and TAN.

"It scans perfectly!"

"I thought it did," said Mum. "I thought it
was lovely."

"Where's your one?" said Sally. "About
Oscar?"

Susan ran her fingers through her hair,
piling it up on the top of her head and letting
it go cascading back down again. She was vain
about her hair.

"I haven't got time to sit around writing
poetry! Some of us have homework to do."

"It only took me an hour," boasted Sally.

"Real poetry would take far longer than
that, and how do you know Fergus is called
O'Dowd?"

" 'Cause I saw it on his collar."

"Well! I just hope he doesn't mind being
put in your poem. His owner, I mean."

"I should think he'd be very proud," said
Mum. "Especially if it wins a prize. I'll go and
pick up an entry form from the pet shop
tomorrow."

On the entry form Sally had to fill in her

age, and her name and address, and the name of the school she went to. As well as the poem, she also had to include a photograph of Beth.

"Mum!" she said. "We haven't got one!"

"We'll get one," promised Mum. "I'll buy a film for the camera."

Next day in school, Sally shyly showed Miss Carpenter the poem she had written. Miss Carpenter said, "My goodness! We have a real poet in our midst. I never knew you could write like this, Sally!"

Sally had never been able to, before. It was Beth who had inspired her.

Miss Carpenter wanted her to read the poem out loud to the class, but Sally was bashful and wouldn't, so Miss Carpenter read it for her. At the end, some of the girls were looking quite weepy.

"It's ever so sad," said one of them, Michelle Walker.

"What's sad?" said Bernard Roberts. "It gets rescued, doesn't it?"

"Yes, but being tied up and left ... I think that's horrible."

All the others agreed that they thought it was horrible, too.

"But she's really happy now," said Gemma. "We took her to the park on Sunday, didn't we?" She turned to a still blushing Sally. "We took her up the park and she *ran*."

"Yes, she did." Sally nodded, proudly. Beth had run because she had seen Fergus. Beth and Fergus were in love. Beth made little excited whimpering noises when they met, and Fergus blew in her ear and nibbled at her ruff. Mr O'Dowd said, "He's really got it bad!"

Sometimes, even now, when Mr O'Dowd did his cuckoo-whistle, Beth would freeze and prick her ears as if old memories were stirring. Sally wished that they knew more about her past. She had several little habits that Mum said must have come from her life before.

Every afternoon at twenty minutes past four almost to the very dot, and even though she had already been to the park with Sally, she would go and sit on the front door mat. Nothing would coax her away; not food, not Minnie or Widget, not Sally herself. It seemed that she had to sit there for a certain length of time – about half an hour – until she was satisfied that she had done her duty.

Another of her habits was to come and place a paw on Sally's knee and whimper softly. For a long time no one had been able to understand what she wanted. At first Mum thought that perhaps she needed to go in the garden, but it wasn't that. Then Sally offered her a dog biscuit, but it wasn't that, either. They tried her with chew sticks and tripe sticks and munchy strips, but it wasn't any of those. And then one day Mum brought home some marrow bone treats, and *that* was what it was.

"She's obviously been spoilt," said Mum; but why would someone spoil a dog and then abandon her?

Nobody knew the answer to that. Mum said, "I'm afraid we probably never shall."

Another of Beth's little habits was sneaking into Sally's bed every night at twelve o'clock and slipping out again at six in the morning. But that was a habit Sally kept to herself!

Mum bought a film for the camera and they

used up the entire roll taking pictures of the dogs. They already had plenty of pictures of Oscar, so he got left out. Not that Oscar cared. He sat on top of the garden shed watching, and every now and again giving one of his enormous yawns. Oscar's yawns were so cavernous that he almost managed to swallow himself. The first time Minnie saw him do it she had rushed excitedly to look inside his mouth. Oscar had almost snapped his jaws shut over her head, so now she was a bit more wary. You had to show respect to a cat like Oscar.

Sally spent almost ten minutes giving Beth a grooming, brushing out her feathers and her long plumy tail. She was anxious that "We've got to take a *good* one, Mum!"

"Let's have some of you both together," said Mum.

When Mum had the film developed next day, they all agreed that the very best one was one that showed Sally kneeling at Beth's side in the garden.

"Nice and natural," said Mum. "Not too posed."

Susan claimed that Sally looked like a garden gnome, but even she had to admit that Beth looked beautiful.

"Old, and wise."

"And intelligent," said Mum.

"And kind," said Sally.

Beth was the gentlest of dogs. She never growled or snapped or showed her teeth. The two little ones could sometimes nip and be quite rough, but not Beth. She was a lady.

She was also, said Mum, a big softie. She let Oscar do just whatever he liked – play with her tail, sit on her head, curl up beside her in one of the dog beds.

"That cat takes advantage rotten," said Mum. "She ought to tell him off occasionally."

"She wouldn't," said Sally. "She's not that sort of dog. Beth is a *good* girl. She's the best!"

"The others certainly have a long way to go," said Mum.

The poem was sent off and Sally forgot all about it. Every afternoon Mum brought Beth to meet her from school and they stopped off for a walk on the way back. Minnie and

Widget went out for an hour and a bit every morning, but Mum said that was too long for a fourteen-year-old dog.

"It's all right now and again, but not every day."

On Saturdays and Sundays, Gemma came over and she and Sally took Beth right across the park to the avenue of trees. This was when she met Fergus.

"Her boyfriend," said Gemma.

"It's as well she's been done," said Mr O'Dowd.

By "done", he meant spayed. Gemma didn't understand what spayed meant – she thought the word was sprayed – so Sally had to explain.

"It means she's had an operation so she can't have babies. Minnie and Widget have, too."

"That doesn't sound very kind," said Gemma.

Sally hadn't thought it was very kind, either, but Mum had said it was far kinder, in the long run, than letting them breed.

"It's sad," said Mum, "but we human

beings have ruined the world for animals. They can't live natural lives any more. That means that we have to look after them and take responsibility for them. If they were all allowed to have puppies the rescue centres would be flooded with thousands of unwanted dogs – and they wouldn't all be as lucky as our three."

"You mean they'd never have homes of their own?" said Sally.

"I mean," said Mum, gravely, "that they would have to be put down."

The thought of it had upset Sally for days.

"Human beings don't get put down," objected Gemma, when Sally told her what Mum had said.

"That's because they're human beings," said Sally. "They can do what they like. It's only animals that can't."

They both agreed that it wasn't fair.

"She probably would have liked to have babies," said Gemma.

"Well, she might have had some," said Sally. "She might have had a litter before she was spayed."

"How do you *know* she's been spayed?"

"You can feel. Down the middle of her tummy ... like a row of bubbles underneath the skin. They're the stitches," said Sally.

Gemma bent down to feel. "Oh, poor Beth!"

"I don't think she minds," said Sally. "Mum says animals don't."

"I still don't think it's fair," said Gemma.

All the people they met in the park – Mr O'Dowd with Fergus, an old lady with a white poodle, a couple with a German shepherd, a lady with two Jack Russells – all agreed that Beth had become "a different dog".

"When I first saw her," said the lady with the Jack Russells, "I thought what a sad old thing she was. All stiff and ribby, and her poor coat so thin. Now look at her! She's positively glowing. You've done a marvellous job!"

"I wonder what her background was?" mused the old lady with the poodle. "I don't think she can have been ill treated or she wouldn't be so calm and good-natured. Somebody must have loved her."

"They can't have loved her very much,"

protested Sally, "or they wouldn't have left her tied to a gatepost!"

"No," said the old lady. "That is a mystery. Why would anyone cherish a dog for fourteen years and then abandon it?"

"Because they're foul," said Gemma; but the old lady seemed to think there must be more to it than that.

"It's possible her owner might have died and she was passed on to someone else. Another member of the family, maybe. And then they discovered they couldn't cope, so they dumped her. I'm afraid," said the old lady, "that people do things like that."

"Mum doesn't think that we shall ever find out," said Sally.

The old lady had to agree that it didn't seem very likely.

One morning, a letter arrived for Ms Sally Barnes. Dad dropped it on the breakfast table, next to Sally's plate.

"A letter?" squeaked Sally. "For me?"

"Looks like it," said Dad. "I believe you are Ms Sally Barnes?"

Who could be writing to her? Sally never

received letters! Only on her birthday, and that was months away.

"You could always try opening it," suggested Susan. "That's what I do, when I get letters; I open them. And then I read what's inside them. But maybe you prefer just to sit and gawp." She leaned across to grab the Shredded Wheat packet. "Oh, well! I suppose we all have our funny little ways."

"I'm *going* to open it," said Sally.

She studied her name and address. She looked at the postmark. Then she turned it over and read, *Top Tins Pet Foods*. She tore at the envelope.

"Don't ruin it!" screeched Susan. Susan was into recycling in a big way. "Oh, you *idiot*! Look what you've done!"

Sally didn't care what she'd done. She pulled out the letter. Her eyes goggled.

"Mum!" she yelled. "I've won!"

Chapter Six

Sally had come top of her section. She had won first prize!

"Fifty pounds of Top Tins," she told Gemma, as they took Beth for her walk on Sunday morning, "and a twenty-pound token to spend in the pet shop."

"It's a pity it's not money," said Gemma, "then you could have bought whatever you wanted."

Sally disagreed.

"I'm going to spend it on Beth. After all, I wouldn't ever have written the poem if it hadn't been for her."

"What are you going to buy her?"

"I'm going to buy her a nice warm coat for

winter. Mum says old dogs feel the cold 'cause they can't run around and keep warm like young ones can. And if there's anything left over I'm going to buy some toys for Minnie and Widget 'cause if it wasn't for them we'd never have gone to the rescue centre in the first place. And me and Mum have decided," said Sally, "that we're going to give them the Top Tins."

"What, the rescue centre?"

"Yes, to help them feed all their dogs. Mum says that we're not desperate, but they are."

"So you won't get a single thing for yourself," said Gemma. "You did all that work, and you're not going to get anything!"

"I am. I'm going to the prize-giving and there's going to be food and we're all going to have our pictures taken for the newspaper. Dad says it's honour and glory," said Sally.

"Sooner have the money," said Gemma; but Sally didn't really care very much about money.

"What would you do if you had lots and lots of it?" said Gemma.

Sally thought.

"I'd start up my own rescue centre for all the poor animals that haven't got homes. What about you?"

"Maybe I'd do that, as well," said Gemma. "I'd go to America *first*, and then I'd come back and start a rescue centre."

"But I wouldn't have them living in cages," said Sally. "I'd have an enormous great house in the middle of a field and they could all walk about and do whatever they wanted."

"They'd all want to come and sleep in your bed!" giggled Gemma. She had heard (and been sworn to secrecy) about Beth climbing into Sally's bed every night. "You'd be smothered under dozens of dogs!"

"I wouldn't mind that," said Sally; and it was perfectly true, she wouldn't.

The prize-giving had been arranged for Saturday morning. Mum and Dad and Sally drove into town to the Top Tins offices, which was where the ceremony was to take place. There they met the other prizewinners, plus the runners-up. Both the other prize-winners, and two of the runners-up, were girls. The 12+ winner had written about her dog Sam, who was a mongrel; the little Under-8 had written about her cat, Blue.

"He's big and fat and sits on the mat
And once Mum found him inside her
hat."

Sally thought that was really good for a seven–year–old.

The others had written about a bouncy boxer dog called Boy, a snow-white kitten called Daz, and a three-legged dog called Fly. The poem about Fly was a bit sad, because Fly had been run over and that was how he had lost his leg, but like Sally's it ended happily:

"Fly can't fly, but he can walk
And almost even run.
But what he likes to do the best
Is bask beneath the sun."

All the poems were read out and everyone applauded. There were lots of parents and important people from Top Tins and a man from the RSPCA (who gave them a talk) and a reporter from the local newspaper.

There was also a photographer who took photographs of the three winners. Sally, remembering what Susan had said about garden gnomes, frowned solemnly at the camera in what she hoped was a dignified fashion, but the photographer wasn't having any of that.

"Smile!" he cried. "That's it, come on ... smile, smile!"

On Wednesday, when the paper arrived through the door along with her dad's *Daily Mail*, Sally was downstairs waiting for it. She snatched it up eagerly before anyone else could get to it and scuttled away into a dark corner.

"She's gone to look at herself!" sang Susan.

So what? She bet Susan would look at herself quickly enough if she ever managed to get into the paper.

The picture was on page 5 – TOP TINS WINNERS! And all of them smiley-smiling as hard as they could go.

Sally studied herself, critically. *Did* she look like a garden gnome? Perhaps she did, just a little bit, with her face all scrunched up and her mouth stretched into a grin. But what was wrong with garden gnomes? The lady next door had a most beautiful one, perched on a mushroom that was red with white spots, and smoking his pipe. Susan said it was dead naff, but Susan said that about most things. She was very hard to please.

"Let's have a look!" Susan had come up and was peering over Sally's shoulder. "Oh, they've printed your poem! Spelling mistakes and all."

"What spelling mistakes?"

"Border," said Susan. "It ought to have an A in it."

"It ought not!" Sally said it indignantly. "Boarder with an A is when you're a boarder. Like at boarding school. Border collie is border like – like in flower beds."

Susan's lip curled. She hated it when Sally was able to set her right about anything.

"What have flower beds got to do with it?"

"*Borders*," said Sally. "*Edges*. Like with countries. Like with—"

"Oh, be quiet! You're boring me." Susan cackled. "I am getting *bored* with *borders*!"

Sally supposed it was quite funny; for Susan.

As well as printing the poems, the newspaper had also printed the photographs of people's animals. There was Sam the mongrel, Blue the big fat cat, Boy the boxer, Daz the kitten, little Fly with three legs – and Beth. Beautiful Beth!

Sally rushed off to show her.

"Look, Beth! You've got your picture in the paper!"

Beth looked and wagged, to show that she was pleased. She was always wagging, these days. Mum said, "It's wonderful to see her so happy. I'd give a lot to know what her past history is."

On Saturday, Mum and Sally went down to the pet shop to spend Sally's twenty-pound token. They bought a splendid red-check waterproof coat for Beth, with a warm fleecy lining, and there was just enough left over to buy a squeaky hedgehog toy for the two little ones.

"That will drive your dad crazy!" laughed Mum.

The squeaky hedgehog drove everyone crazy. Even Sally was almost glad when Minnie put her tooth through it on Sunday afternoon and ruined the squeak once and for all.

On Monday morning, another letter arrived for Ms Sally Barnes. This time it had been sent "C/o The Gazette".

"Fanmail!" said Mum. "Someone must have read your poem."

The letter was short, and written on plain paper without any address. All it said was:

"Her real name is Bess. She was born fourteen years ago, on 11th August. I am so very grateful to you for taking her in and giving her a home. You cannot imagine what a relief this is to me. Bless you, from the bottom of my heart!"

"Why didn't they put their name and address?" wailed Sally. "We could have found things out!"

"Guilty conscience?" said Dad. "They're probably scared you'd have a go at them."

"Well, I would," said Sally, "because what they did was cruel and hateful. But I'd like to ask them things as well!"

"They wouldn't tell you," said Susan. "Not if you'd been rude to them."

"I'd ask them things first and be rude afterwards!"

"No, you would not," said Mum. "If they agreed to see us, it would be extremely impolite."

"Well, but they haven't agreed to see us! They've written an anonymous letter and you shouldn't ever do that." Sally said it virtuously. "It shows they're ashamed."

"They probably are," agreed Mum. "It's obviously been preying on their mind. I wonder if I ought to try ringing the Gazette. . ."

Next Wednesday, on the front page this time, there was a picture of Beth and Sally (the one where Sally looked like a garden gnome) and a big headline:

WHO CAN HELP?

"Sally Barnes, aged $10^3/_4$, winner of Top Tins poetry competition for the 9–11 age group with her poem about Beth, her border collie, would dearly love to know more about Beth's background.

"Beth was rescued by Sally from End of the Road, in Edenbridge, where she had been for three weeks after being found tied to a gate-post with £20 and a note begging them to 'Look after her for me'.

"Mrs Jennifer Barnes, Sally's mum, told the *Gazette*, 'She is a beautiful dog but she is fourteen years old and must have a lot of history behind her. After Sally won the poetry prize we had a most touching note from her previous owner – but unfortunately she did not give us her name and address. If she (or he) would get in touch, we would be so grateful.'"

"Don't get excited," warned Mum. "Nothing may come of it."

"Did she ring?" cried Sally, when Mum met her that afternoon at the school gates.

"I'm afraid not," said Mum.

But the following afternoon...

"Her name is Marion Phillips," said Mum. "She lives in Bromley and she's agreed that we can go and see her on Saturday morning. I have to say that she actually sounds quite nice."

"She can't be," said Sally. "Not after what she did!"

"Just remember that we don't know why she did it. We don't know what lies behind the story."

Sally thought that it didn't matter what lay behind the story; there was no excuse for tying an old dog to a gatepost and leaving her. Marion Phillips had to be hateful, whatever Mum said.

On Saturday morning, Sally and Mum set out in the car for Bromley. Sally had begged to be allowed to take Beth, but Mum said that it wouldn't be wise.

"It might upset her – and it might upset Mrs Phillips, too."

Sally didn't care a 2p piece for Mrs Phillips, but she wouldn't want Beth to be upset.

"She might think she was going back home," said Mum.

Sally crouched by Beth's side.

"You stay here," she whispered. "This is your home now!"

Mrs Phillips lived in an ordinary sort of house rather like the one that Sally lived in. She was an ordinary sort of woman, dressed in a brown skirt and a purple blouse; older than Mum but not as old as Gran, although her hair was grey.

She took Mum and Sally into the sitting-room. It was the neatest, cleanest, tidiest room that Sally had ever seen. In the sitting-room at home there were dogs' toys scattered all about the floor, and piles of books and newspapers, and usually some of Susan's clothes and Susan's homework and bits and pieces of things that Sally was doing for school. Unless Mum had just used the vacuum cleaner there were probably also dogs' hairs on the carpet (and cat's hairs on the furniture). There were dogs lying about in heaps, and Oscar sitting on the window sill (or on the chairs or the sofa or the television).

Mrs Phillips' sitting-room was bare and spotless. Sally perched uncomfortably on the edge of a pale lemon sofa (it wouldn't have stayed pale lemon for five minutes in the Barnes's house).

"Would you care for a cup of something?" said Mrs Phillips. "Tea? Coffee? I'm afraid I don't have anything like orange squash or Coke."

Mum and Sally said they would have some weak tea, please.

"While I'm making it —" Mrs Phillips picked up an envelope from a small spotless table — "you might like to look at these. I went through and picked them out for you. You're welcome to keep them."

In the envelope were photographs of Beth (Sally knew her name was really Bess, but Beth was how she thought of her). There was Beth as a tiny puppy, Beth as a young dog, Beth as she grew older.

"Oh, Mum!" The tears started to Sally's eyes. "I wish we'd had her as a puppy!"

"She was a real charmer, wasn't she?" said Mum.

"We bought her when my son was a baby." Mrs Phillips had come back with two cups of weak tea and one for herself, much stronger. "We thought it would be nice to have them growing up together. This is my son."

She took down a photograph from the mantelpiece. It showed a smiling blond-haired boy, about the same age as Susan.

"That was the last photograph I ever had of him. It was taken on his fourteenth birthday. He died a week later, very suddenly, of meningitis."

A sudden chill fell over the room. Sally squirmed on the edge of the sofa. Mum opened her mouth.

"No, please!" Mrs Phillips held up a hand. It was thin and gnarled, a bit like Gran's, even though she was much younger. "Please don't feel you have to say anything. There's nothing you can say. I just wanted to explain to you – to try and explain to you – why I did – what I did."

She smoothed her hair back off her forehead. It had already been perfectly smooth to begin with. Her hand trembled slightly.

"You see, my husband died a few years ago. Peter – my son – was all I had. We were very close. When I lost him –"

She stopped.

"You don't have to tell us all this," said

97

Mum, gently. "We didn't come to sit in judgement."

"Nevertheless, I should like to tell you, if you can bear it. It would ... ease my conscience. I am deeply ashamed of what I did. In fact, it has haunted me. I have nightmares about it. I feel that Peter, if he knew, would never forgive me. He and Bess were inseparable. He loved that dog so much! And she loved him. Afterwards – when he had gone –"

Her hands, in her lap, were twitching and twisting. Sally looked for reassurance to her mum. She had never seen a grown person this agitated. Mum reached out and patted Sally's knee.

"When he had gone," said Mrs Phillips, "I – I just couldn't stand it! The way she kept padding over to the door and whimpering. Waiting for him. Every afternoon at exactly the same time!"

"Twenty past four?" said Mum.

"Yes. She still does it? It was the time Peter got in from school. He went to the Whitgift, you know, in Croydon." There was pride in Mrs Phillips' voice. "He was a clever boy. He won a scholarship. But of course it was a long way to travel. Bess used to sit, every day, on the front door mat. Every day! Even while he was in hospital – even after he'd – gone. Weeks afterwards! And then at night – up in his room. Just lying there ... waiting!"

Sally sat, with the tears streaming down her cheeks. She wasn't thinking "Poor Mrs Phillips" but "Poor Beth!"

"There," said Mrs Phillips, "I've gone and upset you. I didn't mean to do so. I just wanted you to know ... why I did it. I should not have done it. It is something I shall regret to the end of my days. That was why –" she untwisted her hands, smoothed back her hair – "why I was so relieved when I read your wonderful poem and knew that my Peter, wherever he is, could relax and be at peace. It would have broken his heart to think that Bess was unhappy! You and he would have got on so well."

She smiled, a rather watery smile, at Sally. Sally scrunched her fist into her eyes.

"He was passionate about animals. They were his mission in life. He was going to be a vet when he grew up."

"I'm going to run a rescue centre," said Sally.

"Peter would have approved of that! He always used to say to me, 'Mum, why can't we have another dog? Why can't we go and rescue one?' I used to say, 'Wait till Bess has gone. That's when we'll do it.' But I left it too late."

"We've got three," said Sally. "We got them all from the rescue centre."

"It's what I should have done, years ago. You probably think, 'Stupid old woman! How could she have three dogs? Her house is as neat and as clean as a new pin!' But it never used to be like this. When Peter was here, it was a real, lived-in house. It's only since he's gone – I suddenly can't bear any clutter. I suppose –" she gave a little apologetic laugh – "I suppose I'm trying to shut out my memories, although maybe that's a rather foolish thing to do."

"Memories are very precious," murmured Mum.

"You're right! I know they are. Maybe now that I can stop torturing myself about Bess, I shall be able to find some comfort in them. Anyway!"

She smiled again, bright and nervous. Smoothed at her hair.

"You didn't come to hear about me and my troubles. You want to know about Bess. What can I tell you?"

"Sometimes in the park," said Sally, "we meet a man who whistles like – Mum, you do it! I'm no good at whistling."

Mum pursed her lips and did Mr O'Dowd's cuckoo-whistle.

"It always makes Beth prick her ears up," said Sally. "And once she went running as if – she was expecting someone."

"Yes." Mrs Phillips nodded. "It was how Peter used to whistle her. Sometimes, in the summer, if he was going to be home late – if he had cricket practice, maybe – I would take her into the park and Peter would come and meet us there. He used to stand at the gate and whistle, and she would go running. No matter how far away we were, she always heard him."

"We thought it must be something like that," said Mum.

"Did she sleep in his bedroom?" said Sally.

"Oh, my dear! I'm afraid she did more than that ... she slept in his bed. He never knew that I knew! But of course I did. If you went in at eleven o'clock, she'd be lying in her own bed as good as gold. But I knew that at some point during the night she crept in with him. I saw all the hairs on the sheets! The funny thing was, she was never there in the morning. I always used to take him a cup of tea at half-past six, and there she'd be, back in her own bed, looking as if butter wouldn't melt in her mouth."

"Collies are highly intelligent dogs," said Sally.

"And she was one of the brightest! But you'll have found that out by now. Does she do the same with you? Sneak in after eleven o'clock, sneak out again in the morning?"

Sally's eyes swivelled anxiously in Mum's direction.

"They think we're green as grass," said Mum, "don't they?"

"Mum! She doesn't! She—"

"Oh, now, come on!" said Mum. "I wasn't

born yesterday. Hairs on the sheets—"

"Little muddy patches ... I once asked Peter if he got into bed with his football boots on. The poor boy didn't know which way to look!"

They stayed with Mrs Phillips for almost an hour. When they left, she took both of Sally's hands in hers and said, "Thank you, my dear! Not just for giving a good home to Bess, but for giving me back my memories."

"What did she mean by that?" said Sally, as she and Mum headed back home in the car.

"She meant that she can stop shutting out the past. She can start remembering. It just goes to show," said Mum, "that you shouldn't ever judge people until you know the whole story."

Sally looked rebellious. She could be stubborn when she wanted.

"I still think it was cruel, tying Beth to a gatepost."

"Try to be a little understanding," urged Mum. "Grief can do terrible things to people."

"You mean you'd tie all our dogs to gate-posts if I died of meningitis?" said Sally. "I'd have thought you'd want to keep them more than ever!"

"I think perhaps Mrs Phillips is beginning to wish that she'd kept Beth."

"She's not having her back!"

"No, she's not having her back," said Mum. "In any case, I don't think that Beth would want to go ... she's your dog, now!"

Chapter Seven

Christmas came, and so did Gran: Big Gran, who was Dad's mum. Little Gran lived too far away, in North Wales. They visited her at Easter.

Big Gran always came for Christmas. She was sterner than Little Gran, and she didn't really like dogs. She didn't really like any animals. She had grown used to Oscar, but you could tell that when she looked at Minnie and Widget she wasn't thinking what fun they were but what a *noise* they made, what a *mess* they made. And when she looked at Beth she just saw an old dog with a grey muzzle and a limp. She didn't see how beautiful and kind and intelligent she was.

"It must cost a fortune, feeding all that lot," she said.

"Not really," said Mum. "We've found some excellent vegetarian dog food that they like. Much cheaper than meat."

Gran raised an eyebrow.

"I wouldn't have thought," she said, "that dogs were vegetarians."

"Oh, well, they have a bit of meat. Just now and again. But a heavy meat diet doesn't do anyone any good. Not even dogs."

"Dogs are omnivores." Sally explained it, earnestly. "They can eat anything. Cats are different. They're carnivores; they have to eat meat. Like tigers do. Like—"

"We don't need a *lecture*," said Susan.

"I'm not lecturing. I'm just—"

"Yes, you are! You're lecturing. She's gone dog bananas just lately."

"It's not just lately! I've always been."

"I expect it's just a phase," said Gran. "I seem to remember when I was that age I went through all kinds of phases."

"Yes, like this time last year she was into dinosaurs."

"That was different! Everyone was into dinosaurs." They had done a project on them at school and gone to the Natural History museum to see the models. Sally had bought Gemma a stegosaurus for her Christmas present and Gemma had bought Sally a triceratops.

"The year before that," said Susan, "it was Ninja turtles."

"That was when I was *little*."

"So what do you think you are now?"

"Nearly eleven," said Sally.

"Oh, my!" Gran laughed. "Practically an old age pensioner!"

"Next year it'll be stamp collecting," said Susan. "Or cheese labels, or something."

"No, it will not!"

"Or *phone* cards."

"It will not!"

"How do you know?"

"Well, even if it is," said Sally, "it's not the same! Dinosaurs and stuff are just fun, but dogs –" She paused, not sure how to put it. "Dogs are for *real*."

"So were dinosaurs," said Susan.

"Dinosaurs are extinct. Dogs are *now*."

"Yes, and there are far too many of them, if you ask me," said Gran. She looked across at Dad, trying to enlist his support. "Whatever possessed you?"

"It was me," pleaded Mum. "Entirely my fault."

"And mine!" said Sally. "Mum was the one who wanted Widgie and Min, but I was the one who chose Beth."

"She looks old," said Gran, adjusting her spectacles.

"She's fourteen." Sally said it proudly. Everyone told her these days that Beth was looking like a different dog. "She was fourteen in August."

Gran pursed her lips.

"My neighbour adopted an old dog. Her aunt died and she took the thing over. Everyone warned her not to. She had nothing but trouble from the word go! Running to the vet every five minutes with it. Heart trouble, skin problems, couldn't keep its food down. I dread to think how much it cost her."

"Beth hasn't cost us anything, hardly.

She's only been to the vet once and he said she was perfectly healthy. Didn't he, Mum?"

"He said for her age she was remarkable."

"You wait," said Gran. "You've been lucky so far."

There was a silence.

"Somebody's got to adopt old dogs," said Sally.

"Now, that just isn't true," said Gran. "I have a friend who works for the RSPCA. She says that in most cases it's far kinder to have them put down. There's a lot of sentimentality where animals are concerned," said Gran.

Sally's face had grown quite pink.

"You wouldn't want to be put down!" she said.

"Sally!" Mum tried to sound shocked, but Sally knew when Mum was putting it on. She wasn't really shocked; she was just pretending to be.

"This is what always happens," said Susan. "She gets all het up."

Gran was looking at Sally disapprovingly over her glasses.

"It seems a great pity to me," she said, "that you can't put your energies to better use. There are a lot of human beings who are suffering in this world, you know. You might try thinking of them, for a change."

"I've joined Amnesty International," said Susan; but Gran simply ploughed straight on. She never took any notice of what anyone else said.

"What about all those poor starving people in Ethiopia? I should say they're rather more important than animals, wouldn't you?"

Sally's face, by now, had turned bright scarlet. It was Dad, rather surprisingly, who stepped in and said, "I guess Sally feels there's not a lot she can do for people in Ethiopia."

"She could join Amnesty International," said Susan.

"Well, maybe she will, one day. At the moment she wants to help animals. All of us," said Dad, "can only do what we feel moved to do. Most people don't feel moved to do anything at all."

"I do," said Susan.

She always had to have the last word, but Sally was glad that Dad had stuck up for her. She hadn't thought that he would. Later, when she and Mum were on their own, she said, "Do you think people are more important than animals?"

"Oh, Sally, that's a difficult question!" said Mum. "Don't ask me."

"No, but Mum, *do* you? Really?"

Mum glanced round to make sure no one was listening, then put a finger to her lips and whispered, "No! I think we're equally important. But don't tell your gran!"

On Christmas Day, before everyone opened their presents, Mum and Sally took the dogs for a walk in the park. Beth was wearing her smart new coat, which was just as well as the ground was hard and the air frosty. Minnie and Widget chased sticks to keep warm, but Beth picked her way slowly so that quite often they had to stand and wait for her.

"I expect her arthritis isn't too good in this weather," said Mum.

"Gran has arthritis," said Sally. "She takes pills for it."

"We don't want Beth on pills," said Mum.

"Don't you believe in pills?"

"Not if they're drugs."

"Not *ever*?"

"Only if it's absolutely unavoidable."

When they got back, Sally said to Gran, "Is your arthritis bad in this weather?"

"My arthritis is always bad," said Gran. "I'm starting to fall to pieces."

"Beth has arthritis. But she doesn't take pills for it. Mum doesn't believe in pills. Not if they're drugs."

"No, well, your mum wouldn't," said Gran. "Your mum has some very strange ideas. I suppose she prefers to let the animal suffer."

"Beth doesn't suffer! She's just a bit stiff, that's all. We give her Oil of P— "

Sally stopped, and clapped a hand to her mouth, regarding her mum with horrified eyes. Mum pulled a face and heaved her shoulders up to her ears.

"Oil of Primrose?" Gran said it sharply. "Well, I'm glad you can afford it! I certainly can't."

Sally switched her eyes apprehensively from Mum to Dad; but Dad was over by the Christmas tree, picking up parcels.

"I didn't hear that," said Dad. "Let's get on with opening presents! I want to know what I've got."

Opening presents was always fun, even with Gran there. Mum and Sally, and even Susan, had bought presents for the animals. Oscar had an assortment of catnip mice and kitty strips in a variety of flavours; the dogs had doggy chews and squeaky toys, and nylon bones (chocolate scented) and rubber rings.

Minnie and Widget instantly pounced on their squeaky toys and ran about the room, squeaking them. A pained expression appeared on Gran's face. Good! thought Sally. It served her right. Anyone that said old dogs should be put down deserved to be driven mad by squeaky toys.

Sally had received:

A pair of trainers (from Mum and Dad)
A book about Border Collies (from Mum)

A video of *The Incredible Journey* (from
    Dad)
A jigsaw puzzle with a picture of dogs (from
    Susan)
A calendar with pictures of dogs (from
    Gemma)
A record token (from Auntie Zoë and
    Uncle Jeff)
A book token (from Big Gran)
Another book token (from Little Gran)

"Swop one of your book tokens for my
record token?" she said to Susan.

Susan made the exchange willingly.

"So now you've got twenty-five pounds to
spend on books!" said Gran. "What are you
going to buy?"

"Something about dogs," said Sally.

Having Big Gran in the house was always
what Mum called "a bit fraught". Little Gran
would have been lovely, because Little Gran
was jolly and fun and a bit messy and untidy.
She had hair like a bird's nest and wore old
sweaters and jeans. Also, Little Gran was an

animal person and had six cats and one dog of her own. She wouldn't have minded Minnie and Widget squeaking their toys. She wouldn't have clapped her hands to her ears every time they barked, or pulled a face like a prune when they trailed muddy paw prints across the kitchen floor, or bumped into furniture and knocked coffee cups on to the carpet. She wouldn't even have minded Oscar sitting on the breakfast table and helping himself to food.

Big Gran thought it was dreadful. She kept saying, "Really, Alistair! I don't know how you put up with it," or, "Honestly, Jennifer! That can't be very hygienic."

"I am a sloppy slovenly woman," said Mum to Sally. "And oh, heavens! What has that cat brought in with him?"

"That cat" had obviously been raiding one of the rubbish bags.

"Quick, quick! Whatever it is!" cried Mum. "Before your gran sees!"

Mum and Sally spent all of Christmas on tenterhooks. Beth was the only animal who didn't misbehave. Oscar snatched food and walked on the table, Minnie and Widget ran about the room and knocked things over, but Beth lay quietly in her corner, no trouble to anyone.

"Beth is such a *good* girl," crooned Sally; but Gran remained unmoved. She didn't even smile when Oscar played with Beth's tail or the two little ones used her as a climbing frame.

Sally told her mum that "Gran must have a heart of *stone*."

Mum just sighed and said that some people had no feelings for animals.

"It's like I have no feelings for technology ... show me a computer and I freak."

"I'd rather have animals than computers any day," said Sally.

On the very morning that Gran was due to go home, poor Beth disgraced herself by being sick on the sitting-room carpet. While Mum ran to the kitchen for a bucket and brush and loads of kitchen roll, Sally knelt down to comfort Beth.

"She couldn't help it! It wasn't her fault; you can't always choose where you're going to be sick. I was sick once in the middle of assembly. It's something that just happens."

All Gran said was, "That'll stain the carpet."

Unfortunately it did, just a little bit.

"I'll have to get some carpet shampoo," said Mum.

"Be too late by then. It'll have sunk in."

"Oh, well!" Mum attempted a little laugh. "Children and animals ... you can't be too houseproud."

Sally was more concerned about Beth than about the carpet.

"Do you think she's all right, Mum?"

"Yes, I'm sure she is. Dogs are sick very easily. It's just a pity it had to happen while your gran was here."

"She'd have gone outside if she could," said Sally.

"Of course she would. She's one of the best behaved dogs there is, aren't you, my old darling?"

Beth thumped her tail, but sadly, as if she knew that she had let them down. Or maybe, thought Sally, she wasn't feeling too well.

Maybe she had a tummy ache.

"Be brave," she whispered. "It'll get better."

Next evening, Beth was sick again; in the kitchen, this time.

"Oh, dear!" said Mum. "That's all her dinner she's brought up. You know what the problem is? Too much rich food. Everybody feeding her bits and pieces. She's not used to it."

"Nor are Minnie and Widget," said Sally.

"No, but they're younger, they're more robust. They can cope with it. It's back to normal for you, my girl! No more naughty goodies."

Beth wasn't sick the next day, nor the day after, and Sally stopped worrying. But then one afternoon Mum met her from school and said, "We're taking Beth to the vet. I've made an appointment for ten to four. I thought you'd like to be there with her."

"Mum!" Sally was immediately alarmed. "What's happened?"

"She's been sick again, a couple of times, and she's off her food. I thought we really ought to get her looked at. It's probably only a bit of a bug, but with a dog her age you can't be too careful."

"Oh, Beth!" whispered Sally. "Poor Beth!"

Beth wagged her tail, but very slowly: She certainly didn't seem her normal happy self.

The vet was called Mr Turley. He was old and plump and a bit wheezy, but always comfortable and reassuring. He felt Beth very carefully all over and listened to her heart and looked at her teeth and took her temperature, and finally announced that he could find nothing wrong.

"I'll give her a shot of antibiotic and some tablets to take, and in the meanwhile I should starve her for twenty-four hours then just keep her on a light diet for a day or two. See how she goes."

"*Starve* her?" said Sally, distressed, as she and Mum took Beth back to the car.

"It's only to give her tummy a rest. She won't mind not eating for a day. She doesn't really feel like it at the moment, anyway."

"Can we take her for a walk, Mum?"

"Well ... maybe just a little one. Not too far."

Beth didn't want to go too far; she made that very plain. After only a few minutes, Mum and Sally took her back to the car.

"She's obviously feeling a bit under the weather," said Mum. "Hopefully the antibiotic will help."

"You said you didn't want her to take tablets." Sally reminded her mum of it, reproachfully.

"I wouldn't, as a rule," agreed Mum, "but now and again you don't have much choice. If it were the other two I might just leave them to get over it, but you have to remember that Beth is an old lady. She doesn't have the strength to fight things the way they have."

"Will it work soon, the antibiotic?"

"It should do," said Mum. "Let's get her back home and she can snuggle up in her bed and be quiet."

"Is she all right now?" asked Gemma, when she called round on Sunday to take Beth up to the park.

"She hasn't been sick any more," reported Sally. "But she's still not eating very much."

"I expect her tummy's still a bit funny. Like mine was when I had my grumbling appendix," said Gemma. "I didn't eat anything for a whole week, hardly. Just drank lemon barley water."

"Beth's having soya milk," said Sally.

"Is that good for her?"

"Mum says it is. But I hope she gets all right again soon!"

January turned into February, and with February came bitterly cold weather and driving sleet and rain. Beth wasn't too keen to go out any more. Mum still brought her to meet Sally from school but now she left her in the car, and they didn't stop off on the way home to give her a walk. She spent most of her time these days lying in front of the fire, not asleep but just staring into space. At twenty minutes past four, with a weary sigh, she would dutifully heave herself up and go trundling off to sit on the front-door mat, but Mum said, "I'm not sure, any more, that she

121

knows why she's doing it. It's just a habit."

One Sunday when the rain had stopped, Gemma called round and they dressed Beth in her nice warm coat and took her up to the park.

"Don't go too far with her," said Mum. "Remember, she's an old lady."

It took them a long time to reach the park.

"It's like walking with my nan," said Gemma. "You just have to crawl everywhere. It's because of her joints. They've all worn out."

"Beth will be all right when it's warm," said Sally. "She just doesn't like the cold weather."

"Old people don't," said Gemma. "They feel it in their bones. That's what my nan says."

It was what Beth would have said, thought Sally, if only she could talk.

"We'll just go halfway to the avenue and then come back," she said; but before they had gone even halfway, Beth had given up. She sank to the ground and wouldn't move, no matter how Sally coaxed and pleaded.

"What's the matter with her?" cried Gemma.

"I don't know!" Sally was in tears. "How are we going to get her home?"

She was too heavy for either of them to carry. Gemma was just suggesting that maybe they could manage her between them when Mr O'Dowd appeared through the trees with Fergus.

"Hallo!" he said. "What's the problem?"

"It's Beth," sobbed Sally. "She can't walk!"

Mr O'Dowd was a great deal bigger and stronger than either Sally or Gemma. He said that if one of them would take Fergus on the lead when they reached the park gates, he would carry Beth home.

Once she was indoors, by the fire, Beth seemed to recover. She thumped her tail when Sally stroked her and covered her face in apologetic licks. But she didn't want to eat; she wouldn't even drink a saucer of milk.

"Mum, what do you think's the matter with her?" asked Sally.

"Darling, I don't know," said Mum. "I suspect she's just terribly tired."

"You mean, she needs a rest," said Sally.

"She does," said Mum. "A long rest."

"And then she'll be all right again?"

"We'll see, sweetheart. We'll see."

That night when Sally went to bed, Dad had to carry Beth up the stairs; and when she whimpered as usual at midnight, and Sally, eyes glued together with sleep, held up the duvet, she couldn't find the strength to jump. Sally had to scramble out of bed and help her.

When Mum came in to wake her at seven o'clock, Beth was still in the bed, fast asleep.

"Don't bring her to meet me after school," said Sally. "I'd rather she had a rest."

But Mum did bring her, because, she said, Beth insisted.

"She wouldn't let me go without her. It's the highlight of her day, meeting you from school."

And then she told Sally that that morning she had taken Beth back to the vet and that the vet had taken a blood sample.

"We have to find out what's wrong with her, Sal."

"She just needs a rest," said Sally. "That's all!"

"It might just be that, but it might be something more. It might be something the vet can treat her for."

"Like he might be able to give her a tonic," said Susan, when Mum told her and Dad about it over supper.

"When will the results come through?" Dad wanted to know.

"He thinks in a day or two."

"Did he –" Dad paused. "Did he give you any idea what it might be?"

Sally caught just the faintest of frowns on Mum's brow as she quickly shook her head and said, "No. He said it could be any one of a number of things."

"Not bad things?" begged Sally. "Mum, not bad things?"

"Let's hope not," said Mum.

Next day at school, Sally told Gemma about the blood test.

Gemma said, "My nan had a blood test."

Gemma's nan had had everything. "My *old* nan. They said she was – something or other. I can't remember what it's called. It meant her blood wasn't red enough, so they gave her these tablets and then it got all right again. Maybe they could do that with Beth. Give her tablets to make her blood go red."

"It's just she needs a rest," said Sally. "That's all."

At breaktime Miss Carpenter called to Sally to stay behind. She said, "Gemma tells me you're worried about Beth."

"She's had to have a blood test," said Sally.

"Well, I hope it isn't anything serious," said Miss Carpenter, "but she is a very old doggie, isn't she? I had a dog like that when I was young. She lived to be almost fifteen. I cried and cried when we lost her, so I do know how upsetting it is. I'm afraid it's all part of the pain of owning these lovely little people. They have such short lives. But while they're with us, they give us so much pleasure. So that's what you must think about, and try not to be too sad."

Sally tilted her chin.

"Beth's all right," she said. "She just needs a rest, that's all."

Next day when Mum came to meet Sally from school it was snowing, and she didn't have Beth in the car.

"It was too cold to bring her out. I left her tucked up in her bed."

Sally's lip quivered.

"Didn't she want to come?"

"She tried to, but it's such an effort for her. I think she was quite grateful when I told her to stay."

When they arrived home, Beth's tail thumped but she stayed where she was, in her bed in the corner of the kitchen.

Mum said, "Sally, darling, I want you to be very brave."

She took both Sally's hands in hers. "We had the results of the blood test today. Beth has a tumour in her liver. She's a very sick dog, Sally. She's not in any pain, but we have to face it, sweetheart, she's not going to get any better."

Sally stood, frozen like a statue.

"I took her up there this morning and the

vet examined her. He said that quite honestly the kindest thing to do would be to put her to sleep."

The tears started to Sally's eyes.

"He offered to do it right away, but I said I couldn't let that happen. I said that she was your dog, and that we couldn't let her go without you saying goodbye. And also, it has to be your decision."

"I don't want her put to sleep!"

"Darling, I know you don't. I don't, either." Mum was crying as well, now. "But we have to think of Beth, not of ourselves. If she's no longer enjoying life –"

"She is! She wagged at me!"

"Yes, because she loves you very dearly. But she can't go for walks any more, she's not eating, she's very weak and she's desperately tired. We can't just let her linger. I know that it's the most terrible decision for you to make, I know that it seems unspeakable, almost like a betrayal, but it's not a betrayal, Sally! It's doing our duty by her.

"You promised her, when we took her from the kennels, that you would love her and look after her. Well, this is the hardest part of loving . . . knowing when the time has come to let go. Being brave enough. For her sake. Because it would be cruel, Sally, to let her linger on to the very end."

Sally stood, with the tears pouring unchecked down her cheeks.

"Think about it," said Mum. "Don't try to make any decision immediately. See how you feel in the morning."

Chapter Eight

It was Mum who carried Beth upstairs that night. Gently, she laid her on Sally's bed.

"Try to get some sleep," she told Sally. "We'll talk about things in the morning."

A few minutes after Mum had gone, Dad came into the room.

"Sal?" He sat on the edge of the bed and took one of Sally's hands. "You all right?"

Tears welled in Sally's eyes. She shook her head.

"I know," said Dad. "I know. It's bad news." He leaned across and ruffled Beth's fur. "Even I've gone and got fond of her. I never thought I would; I never thought I was a dog person. But you won me over, didn't you, old lady?"

Beth's tail thumped, very faintly, under the duvet.

"The thing is, Sal ... it's something we all have to face, sooner or later. Your mum had to face her little dog dying, when she was a girl. Your gran – your mum's gran – you know she's got a whole graveyard in her back garden. All the dogs and cats that have come and gone. It's never easy. You get attached to them, it's hard to let them go. But when the time is right—"

"It's not!" cried Sally. "Not yet!"

"No. Well..." Her dad squeezed her hand. "I'm just saying ... when it is, I know you'll do the right thing. Mm?"

Sally nodded, her tears spilling over on to the pillow.

"That's my girl!"

Dad gave her hand a final squeeze and was gone. He hadn't said a word about dogs sleeping in beds.

Sally lay cuddled up, her arms around Beth, her face buried in Beth's ruff.

"Please don't go yet, Beth," she whispered. "I don't want you to go yet!"

That night, Sally had a dream. She dreamt that Beth was a young dog, springing and jumping as only a young dog can. She was in a garden – a garden that Sally had never seen before – playing in the bright sunshine with a little boy who had fair hair. The boy seemed familiar, even though the garden wasn't. She realized in her dream that it was Peter, when he was younger. He was throwing a ball and Beth was catching it. High into the air she leapt, full of joy and the love of living.

And then the scene changed. The sun went in and the clouds gathered. Peter faded, became transparent, disappeared altogether, even as the garden began to look more familiar, with trees and shrubs and bushes. Now it was the garden of Sally's own house, and there was Beth, an old dog, lying in her favourite spot beneath the flowering currant.

Suddenly, in the dream, there came the sound of a whistle. Beth cocked her head, her ears pricked. The whistle came again. It seemed to come from somewhere beyond the back gate.

Beth dragged herself painfully to her feet. Slowly, with her collie's characteristic walk, low to the ground, slinking, like a fox, she made her way to the gate.

The whistle came for the third time. Sally watched, in her dream, as Beth attempted to gather her forces and spring; but she was an old dog now. She no longer had the strength. She sank to her haunches by the gate, and whimpered.

That was when Sally woke. She found Beth sitting upright in the bed. She was trembling.

"Beth?" Sally put both her arms round her. "What is it, Beth?"

Beth whimpered, pitifully. She looked at Sally with eyes that seemed to plead. What was she asking for? What did she want?

Sally knew what she wanted. She was saying, just as plainly as she could, "Please! Let me go."

Next morning, when Mum came in to wake her, Sally was already dressed and out of bed.

"Mum, I've decided," she said.

"What's that, darling?"

Sally pushed her hair back behind her ears. In a tight, controlled voice she said, "It's time for Beth to go. She wants to. She told me. It wouldn't be kind –" her voice suddenly cracked – "it wouldn't be kind to keep her any longer!"

"Oh, Sally!" Mum sank on to the bed and folded Sally into her arms. "You are a very brave girl! I knew that you would be. And it is the right decision."

"I know!" sobbed Sally. "But, Mum, I love her so!"

"It's because you love her that you're letting her go," said Mum. "Because it would be cruel to let her suffer. Let's carry her downstairs and put her in her bed in the kitchen."

They were all in tears as they sat round the breakfast table. Dad blew his nose very hard into his handkerchief. Even Susan was red-eyed and weepy.

"I knew this would happen," said Susan. "I knew you shouldn't have got an old dog."

"Susan, don't be unkind," said Mum.

"I'm not being unkind!" Susan blotted at her eyes. "But it's just so *miserable*! How can I go to school looking like this?"

"I feel a right berk," said Dad. "A grown man in tears over a dog."

"And why not?" Mum said it fiercely. "She's one of the family!"

"We've only had her a few months," said Susan.

"Yes, but they were good months! For us and for her." Mum reached out and took Sally's hand. "It's been worth it," she said. "Every minute of it."

"She wouldn't have liked it if she'd been left in the kennels, Mum, would she?"

"She would have hated it," said Mum.

"And she has been happy with us, hasn't she?"

"She's had a wonderful time!"

"And she's not suffering, Mum, is she?"

"No, darling, she's not suffering. She's just very old and very tired, and it's time for us to let her rest."

Mum said that she would ring the vet and ask him to call round.

"I know it costs more than taking her up to the surgery, but she ought to be allowed to go to sleep in her own home. We owe her that much."

Dad said Mum must do whatever she thought best.

"You can't worry about expense at a time like this."

Susan actually bent down to kiss Beth goodbye – and then ran out of the house, very quickly, with red eyes and her face all scrunched up.

"Mum, I don't have to go to school, do I?" asked Sally. "Please, Mum! I want to be here with her!"

Mum hesitated. She said, "Sally, darling, I think you'll find it upsetting."

"But she's my dog! I have to be with her!"

In the end, Mum gave way. She promised that she would ring the school and say Sally wasn't very well.

"I know it's not strictly the truth but I don't think a little white lie hurts just now and again. You won't want everyone knowing what's happened. Not until you've had a chance to get over it."

"I won't ever get over it!" wept Sally.

"You will, darling. You will! I promise. One day you'll look back and all your memories will be happy ones. But for the moment, we've both of us got to be brave. We've got to remind ourselves that we're doing this for Beth's sake. We're the ones who are going to suffer, not her. And that's the way it should be," said Mum, "isn't it?"

They left Beth curled up in her bed and took Minnie and Widget along to the park. Minnie and Widget obviously knew that Beth was not well for they both left her alone. Only Oscar crept up and gently sniffed at her, then lay down by her side.

"Oscar's going to miss her," said Sally.

"We shall all miss her," said Mum. "She's going to leave one great big hole. It's funny how even your dad took to her."

"That's because she's a very special dog."

"She is," agreed Mum. "There's no doubt about that."

In the park they met Mr O'Dowd and Fergus.

"Hallo!" said Mr O'Dowd. "Not at school today?"

"No," said Sally, and went racing ahead with Minnie and Widget before he could ask her why not. When Mum caught up with her again, Sally said, "Did you tell him?"

"Yes, I had to," said Mum. "He was very sympathetic. That's the nice thing about dog people ... they all understand how you're feeling. They don't think it's silly or sentimental."

"Poor Fergus! He won't have a girlfriend any more."

"Fergus is still a young man. He'll find himself another one. But wasn't it lovely for Beth," said Mum, "that she should have had a gentleman admirer in her old age? You wait till I tell your gran ... how jealous she'll be!"

"Why?" said Sally. "Would Gran like a gentleman admirer?"

"I don't expect she'd say no! Animal Gran, that is."

Sally thought about it, as she threw sticks

for the two little ones. Animal Gran was lovely, but she wasn't as beautiful as Beth. She said so to Mum, and Mum laughed.

"I won't tell her *that*," she said.

Mr Turley, the vet, came after lunch. He said to Sally, "You're obviously a person who cares very deeply about animals. You're thinking of Beth rather than of yourself. I only wish all my clients were like that! Maybe you'll be a vet when you grow up. Have you ever considered it?"

Sally hadn't. A vet was what Peter had been going to be.

"Give it some thought," said Mr Turley. "The animals need people like you."

He told Sally she could hold Beth if she wanted.

"She won't feel a thing, I promise you. You just sit there and stroke her and she'll slide away so peacefully you won't even know that it's happening."

Sally buried her face in Beth's fur.

"Goodbye, darling Beth," she whispered. "I love you!"

Beth's tail thumped just once, and then it

was over. Peacefully, as Mr Turley had promised.

"There," he said. "She's all right, now."

Afterwards, Mum and Sally cried and cried. Mum said that really they shouldn't, because Beth after all was happy, but neither of them could help it.

"We have to get it out of our systems," wept Mum.

Dad came home early, at three o'clock, before it grew dark. He went into the garden and dug beneath the snow in the hard earth; and then they wrapped Beth in a blanket – "So she won't be cold," said Sally – and buried her in her favourite spot beneath the flowering currant.

"We mustn't be sad," said Mum; but they were, all the same.

"Why don't we go up the road for a pizza?" suggested Dad. "And then we'll get out a video. Something jolly, to take our minds off things."

They took out two videos, because Dad and Susan couldn't agree. Dad wanted Walt Disney, Susan wanted *Batman*, so in the end they took them both and stayed up until midnight watching them. Sally was almost never allowed to stay up until midnight. She knew why Mum had let her. Partly it was because it was Friday and there wasn't any school tomorrow, but mostly it was because she wanted Sally to be tired, so that she would go to sleep and not lie awake all night thinking about Beth.

Sally was quite sure that she *would* lie awake, but in fact she was so worn out with weeping that she fell asleep almost as soon as her head touched the pillow.

She might have slept right through till morning if a sound from outside hadn't woken her. She lay for a moment, listening. What was it? What had she heard?

And then she heard it again ... a whistle! Beth's whistle!

Sally scrambled out of bed and ran across to the window. The winter sky was dark and starless, but the light of a large pot-bellied moon flooded the garden, cold and bright and silver.

From under the flowering currant trotted

a black shape, tail held low like a fox's brush. It reached the gate at the end of the path, and there it paused and looked back. Looked straight up at Sally's window. Just for a second, it seemed to hesitate, as if unsure what to do. Whether to go – or whether to stay.

The whistle came a third time, loud and clear in the stillness of the night.

Sally raised a hand in final farewell.

"Go, Beth! He's calling you!"

She watched, nose pressed to the glass, as the black shape gathered its forces and leapt at the gate, hauled itself up and over, and disappeared into the night.

Beth and Peter were together again.

Next morning, at breakfast, Susan said, "There was a fox in the garden last night. I heard Minnie and Widget barking and I looked out of the window and I saw it. It went over the back gate."

Sally didn't say anything, but after breakfast she went into the garden with Minnie and Widget. They had already been out there, earlier; she could see where they had churned up the snow. But they hadn't been as far as the flowering currant. They had only chased about near the house, biting and pouncing as they always did when first let out.

From the flowering currant to the back gate there was a trail of footprints.

"See?" said Susan, who had followed Sally out. "I told you! A fox."

A fox that was lame on its right back leg . . .

"Goodbye, Beth!" whispered Sally.

That afternoon, Mum said, "It's your birthday next month, Sal. Let's try and be cheerful! What do you want?"

Sally said, "Can I have *whatever* I want?"

"Well – I should think so. Within reason. If it doesn't cost too much."

"How much would be too much?"

"How much were you thinking of?"

"About . . . thirty pounds, maybe." Thirty pounds was what Mum had paid for Minnie and Widget.

"I should think we might be able to run to that. Tell us what you'd like."

Sally took a breath.

"What I would like – what I would *really* like –"

"Yes?"

"What I would *really* like is for us to go back to the rescue centre and rescue another poor dog."

There was a long silence. Mum looked at Dad. Dad, hastily, snatched up his paper.

"Not another old one," begged Susan. "Please! I couldn't bear it!"

"One that nobody else wants," said Sally. "Like if they had one that wasn't very pretty, or was deaf, or only had three legs, or – or maybe was *quite* old. Because I do think," said Sally, "that people that are animal people ought to do these things. Otherwise all these poor dogs won't ever have homes. And I did learn to let go, didn't I, Mum? You didn't think I would, but I did!"

"Yes, you did," said Mum. "That's quite true."

"So can we, Mum? Can we go back and rescue another one?"

"What about Beth?" said Susan. "It's being disloyal."

"No, it isn't." Sally had spent all morning thinking about this. "Beth was a *kind* dog. She'd be happy to think we were rescuing someone else. Please, Mum! Say we can!"

Weakly, Mum said, "You'd better ask your dad."

"Dad?" said Sally. "*Can* we?"

"I don't know why you bother to consult me," said Dad. "You and your mum just seem to do whatever you like."

"Does that mean yes?" cried Sally. "Oh, *Dad*!" She flung herself at him. "You are the very *best* Dad in the whole wide world!"

"I'll only say one thing," said Dad. "No Rottweilers –"

"No, Dad."

"No Wolfhounds –"

"*No*, Dad."

"No Bull Mastiffs –"

"*No*, Dad!"

"That's three things," said Susan.

"All right, so here's a fourth ... one dog and one dog only. Do I have your promise?"

Sally beamed. "*Yes*, Dad!"

HIPPO ANiMAL

Have you ever longed for a puppy to love, or a horse of your own? Have you ever wondered what it would be like to make friends with a wild animal? If so, then you're sure to fall in love with these fantastic titles from Hippo Animal!

Owl Cry
Deborah van der Beek
Can Solomon really look after an abandoned baby owl?

Thunderfoot
Deborah van der Beek
When Mel finds the enormous, neglected horse Thunderfoot, she doesn't know it will change her life for ever...

Vanilla Fudge
Deborah van der Beek
When Lizzie and Hannah fall in love with the same dog, neither of them will give up without a fight...

A Foxcub Named Freedom
Brenda Jobling
An injured vixen nudges her young son away from her. She can sense danger and cares nothing for herself – only for her son's freedom...

Goose on the Run

Brenda Jobling

It's an unusual pet – an injured Canada goose.
But soon Josh can't imagine being without him.
And the goose won't let *anyone* take him away
from Josh...

Pirate the Seal

Brenda Jobling

Ryan's always been lonely – but then he meets
Pirate and at last he has a real friend...

Animal Rescue

Bette Paul

Can Tessa help save the badgers of Delves Wood
from destruction?

Take Six Kittens

Bette Paul

James and Jenny's dad promises them a pet when
they move to the country. But they end up with
more than they bargained for...

Take Six Puppies

Bette Paul

Anna knows she shouldn't get attached to the
six new puppies at the Millington Farm Dog
Sanctuary, but surely it can't hurt to get just a
little bit fond of them...

HIPPO GHOST

Secrets from the past... Danger in the present...
Hippo Ghost brings you the spookiest of tales...

R.L. Stine

Reader beware, you're in for a scare!

These terrifying tales will send shivers up your spine:

Goosebumps

Goosebumps

Reader beware – here's THREE TIMES the scare!

Look out for these bumper GOOSEBUMPS editions. With three spine-tingling stories by R.L. Stine in each book, get ready for three times the thrill … three times the scare … three times the GOOSEBUMPS!

Elizabeth Lindsay

Ride into adventure with Mory and her pony,
Midnight Dancer

Book 1: Midnight Dancer
Mory is thrilled when she finds the perfect pony.
But will she be allowed to keep her?

Book 2: Midnight Dancer: To Catch a Thief
There's a thief with his eye on Mory's mother's sapphire
necklace – and it's down to Mory and Midnight Dancer
to save the day…

Book 3: Midnight Dancer: Running Free
Mory and Dancer have a competition to win. But they
also have a mystery to solve…

Book 4: Midnight Dancer: Fireraisers
There's trouble on Uncle Glyn's farm – because there's
a camper who loves playing with fire. Can Mory and
Dancer avert disaster?

Book 5: Midnight Dancer: Joyriders
Mory's rival, Caroline, has her twin cousins to stay.
And they look like trouble. . .

Book 6: Midnight Dancer: Ride By Night
Sheep are disappearing from the hillsides; and Mory
and Midnight Dancer are determined to help. . .